The MASK OF ARIBELLA

ANNA HOGHTON

Chicken House

2 Palmer Street, Frome, Somerset BA11 1DS
www.chickenhousebooks.com

Text © Anna Hoghton 2020
Cover illustration © Paola Escobar 2020

First published in Great Britain in 2020
Chicken House
2 Palmer Street
Frome, Somerset BA11 1DS
United Kingdom
www.chickenhousebooks.com

Cover and interior design by Helen Crawford-White
Cover illustration by Paola Escobar
Typeset by Dorchester Typesetting Group Ltd
Printed and bound in Great Britain by CPI Group (UK) Ltd, Croydon CR0 4YY

The paper used in this Chicken House book is made from
wood grown in sustainable forests.

1 3 5 7 9 10 8 6 4 2

British Library Cataloguing in Publication data available.

PB ISBN 978-1-912626-10-6
eISBN 978-1-912626-58-8

To Matt and Sue

'Magic is believing in yourself. If you can do that, you can make anything happen.'

Johann Wolfgang von Goethe

1

Aribella and her friend Theo sat side by side on the deck of the fishing boat, looking out across the lagoon to their island home. Already Burano's brightly coloured cottages were dissolving into the distance. It was the last morning of September, the day before Aribella's thirteenth birthday.

'Aren't you going to help?' Theo's papa called, struggling with the sail. 'The others are leaving us behind.'

Theo rolled his eyes but sprang to his feet.

Aribella stayed where she was. Girls were bad luck on boats, so fishing folk said. Thankfully, Theo's papa wasn't as superstitious as the rest of them and allowed Aribella on board, but he drew the line at her handling the sail. Since he was already doing her a kindness, she did not complain. All the same, she watched Theo keenly as he wrestled with the ropes, trying to learn as much as she could.

The dirty old sail whipped about the creaking mast, then billowed and caught. Theo let out a small whoop of triumph.

'*Bravo!*' his papa called, angling the rudder.

The ancient fishing boat began to move smoothly across the dark water, gathering momentum, and soon joined the small fleet sailing towards the main island of Venice.

Sleepy-eyed boys regarded Aribella warily from the decks of the other boats. She dropped her gaze, used to these sorts of looks.

Theo flopped back down beside her. 'Still don't get why you wanna come,' he said, dipping the toe of his boot into the passing water. 'I *have* to, but you – you could spend the morning exploring rooftops, or playing with Luna, or swimming, or—'

'I like coming,' Aribella interrupted, wrapping her cloak round her body.

Theo snorted. 'No one *likes* getting covered in fish guts.'

'I don't mind it,' she insisted.

'Suit yourself,' Theo scoffed, but he was smiling.

The lagoon and sky lightened to orange and pink.

The world was soft and hazy, like the edge of a dream. Other fishermen called greetings to Theo's papa, which he returned cheerily. Aribella felt a tug of yearning as she looked up at his open, bearded face. He was so bright and full of life, so unlike her father.

Aribella loved helping at the fish market – the *pescheria* – because, just for a short while, it made her feel that she was part of something, that she belonged. And though she felt guilty for admitting it, she relished the excuse to be out of Papa's gloomy house, where he sat, day after day, making his beautiful lace in silent mourning. It had been ten years since Mama passed but Papa had never recovered. Aribella had been an infant and could barely remember her. She worried about Papa constantly, except at the market, where she was so busy she could forget for a while – though she'd feel bad about that afterwards.

Theo leant back on his elbows and closed his eyes. Aribella kept hers open, gazing at the other islands as they floated by. There was Sant' Erasmo, dotted with farms that produced fruit and vegetables for the whole city. Some Burano boys had once tried to steal artichokes there and been chased off with sticks. Lots more boats were setting off from the island's jetty, on their way to market. Next was Murano, the renowned glass-blowers' island, and then San Michele, the cemetery island.

3

Gulls cried on the horizon and the sun slid out of the lagoon. Thin trails of pale blue ribboned the sky and the main island of Venice came dazzlingly into view.

Piazza San Marco was already full of crowds. The rising sun shone off the red brick of the bell tower, the *campanile,* and the pale walls of the Doge's palace gleamed. It was low and rectangular, decorated like the most beautiful cake, with a pattern of stone arches that were as intricate as Papa's lace. Rows of dark windows looked out towards the lagoon like the eyeholes of a Venetian mask.

As their boat got closer, she made out the carving of the head of a lion in the palace wall, its jaws open. The Lion's Mouth. She was too far away to read the inscription engraved underneath, but she knew what it said. Even children who couldn't read knew: *Per Denontie Segrete* – 'For Secret Accusations'.

Parents warned naughty children that their names would be put into the Lion's Mouth and the Doge's guards would come and punish them . . . Of course it wasn't really for disobedient children. Anyone seen as dangerous could have their name placed in the Lion's Mouth at any time, by *anyone.* No one knew what happened to them after the guards came. Some said they were thrown into the palace prison. Others, that they were hanged between the columns in Piazza San

Marco in the dead of night . . .

One thing was for sure: you didn't want to find out. Aribella shivered.

'Hello? Aribella?' Theo waved a hand in front of her eyes.

'Sorry. I was miles away.' She smiled. 'What were you saying?'

But whatever it was, was forgotten, because the next instant Theo jumped to his feet, making the boat rock, and pointed, shouting, '*Santo cielo!* It's the Doge.'

Sure enough, sweeping ahead of them, moving far faster than the fishing boats, was a fleet of elegant gondolas, steered by masked palace guards. And seated in the middle gondola, recognizable by his snow-white robes and glittering diamond mask, was the Doge of Venice.

Aribella jumped to her feet too. The Doge had not been seen outside the palace for months and had been ill for years. A cheer rose up as he raised a gloved hand and waved. He had always been generous to the poor, at least before he fell ill.

'Good to see him up and about,' said Theo's papa.

The Doge turned towards them, and his jewelled mask flashed blindingly in the sun so that Aribella had to close her eyes. When she opened them again, the Doge had turned back towards the palace.

'Do you think he wears the mask to hide how poorly he is?' she asked Theo.

Theo shrugged. 'Maybe. I remember seeing him when I was little and I swear he didn't wear a mask then. You weren't even born,' he teased, adding, 'He probably just likes it. If I owned a mask with that many jewels on, I'd wear it all the time too. Though it's not his mask I'd want—'

'It's the gondolas,' Aribella finished.

Theo smiled. 'Just look at them – they're so fast! Do you know that they're made from several different types of wood? Oak, cherry, elm, pine . . .'

As a matter of fact, Aribella did know because Theo had already told her – many times.

'And they're deliberately lop-sided to counter-balance the weight of the rower at the back,' he continued. 'And that curved bit at the front – that's called the *ferro*. Isn't it, Papa? Oh, I'd love to own a gondola one day.' Theo sighed wistfully.

Theo's papa rolled his eyes and ignored him.

'Maybe you will,' Aribella said encouragingly.

Theo only sighed again and Aribella regretted her words. She knew what Theo was thinking: only those born into rich Venetian families got to own gondolas. Theo would be a fisherman all his life, like his father and grandfather before him. Still, at least he knew his place in the world. Aribella envied the clearness of his path. Her own was as murky as canal water.

The palace fleet reached the jetty. The Doge stepped from his gondola and disappeared through an archway into the palace, followed by his guards. A few fishermen let out groans of disappointment to see him go, calling out wishes for his good health. The fishing boats swung away from the palace, moved past the *campanile* and entered the Grand Canal, the main waterway of the city, which snaked in an S-shaped curve through the main island. This morning, as on all mornings except Sundays, it was a sparkling ribbon of activity, packed with trading boats laden with wares: bright tomatoes and flashing sardines among them.

More traders called greetings to Theo's papa.

'*Ciao! Buongiorno!*' Theo's papa called back, and Aribella glowed with pride just to be on the same boat.

She gazed up at the grand palazzos either side of the Grand Canal that were the homes of Venice's richest families. The flower-covered balconies, beautiful jetties and arched entrances were a world away from the higgledy-piggledy cottages on Burano. Many were worthy rivals to the Doge's palace itself, and the sun slid from window to window as if it couldn't decide which to stay in. Aribella and Theo spent many morning journeys fantasizing about what it might be like to live in a palazzo. Theo always teased Aribella about her favourite, which was halfway along the Grand Canal, just before the Rialto Bridge. The orange-and-purple stained-glass doors were smashed and boarded up, and the canary-yellow paint was peeling. It was a wonder it hadn't been torn down, but Aribella was glad it hadn't. There was just something about it that she liked.

The world was suddenly cold and dark as their fishing boat slipped into the shadow beneath the Rialto Bridge. Aribella and Theo played their usual game of touching the underside with their fingers. It had seemed so tricky when they were young and small, but now they could both reach the slimy bricks with ease.

It reminded Aribella that her days following Theo to the market were numbered. Thirteen was considered an adult by some. Theo was going to be a fisherman but what would she become? A lacemaker like Papa? She was clumsy and awful at sewing, but how else would she and Papa survive when his eyesight worsened, as it surely would?

She pushed these worries from her mind as they emerged back into the bright sunshine on the other side of the bridge. As usual, she caught the smell of the *pescheria* – a pungent, salty odour that she'd grown to love – even before she saw the colourful mishmash of stalls crammed under the arches of the loggia.

Theo's papa docked the boat on the traders' jetty and went ahead to set up the stall, leaving Aribella and Theo to unload the fish. The crates were half-empty today, just as they had been all year. The recent decline of fish in the lagoon was making every family on Burano anxious. No one could afford to lose money.

'Bad catch again this week,' Theo muttered.

'Everyone's in the same boat,' a nearby fisherman remarked. 'Must be a change in the swell or something.'

'Pah!' called another, his expression dark. 'It's been eight months of this! I'll tell you the real reason. Fortune teller said a blood moon's comin'. And you know what that means.'

'What?' asked the first fisherman.

'It's a bad omen. Very bad indeed.' The second man gave Aribella a suspicious look she pretended not to see.

2

'What's a blood moon?' Aribella muttered to Theo as they carried the crates away.

'No idea, just some rubbish.' He shrugged. Like his papa, Theo didn't have time for folk tales and other 'superstitious nonsense'. 'That man wastes all his family's bread money on fortune tellers and palm readers, Papa told me,' he added dismissively.

Palm readers were always robbing fishermen of their hard-earned coins. But she couldn't get the way the man had stared at her out of her head. She was used to dirty looks from other children, but the adults usually let her be.

Aribella tried not to think about it and concentrated on working hard instead.

It turned out to be a fun morning. She and Theo

prepared all the fish, and sold a decent amount too. Theo made her laugh by pretending a lobster was alive and dancing it across the table. At lunchtime, his papa brought them warm bread rolls and they sat down on the cold stone of the canal-side to eat, their legs dangling over the water. The canal smelt a great deal better in autumn than in summer, and though it was chilly, it was pleasant sitting there in the sunshine with Theo.

'Are you and your papa doing anything nice tomorrow?' he asked.

'No. Why?' Aribella asked.

'Because it's your birthday, of course! Thirteen is a big one, you know.'

'Oh.' Aribella flushed. She'd almost forgotten and Papa wasn't likely to remember either. When she was little, Papa would buy her a slice of cake to mark the day, but as she'd grown older he'd stopped. It was as if each birthday reminded him that yet another year had passed without Mama.

'Nothing planned,' she muttered hastily. 'You know how he is.'

'Is he still sad?' Theo asked. 'Sorry, I just mean . . . well, it's been ten years.'

'I know. But if anything he's getting worse.' She looked away, swallowing hard. If she thought about it too much it made her eyes sting.

'Sorry, Ari. I don't mean to upset you . . . I only mean that maybe you could remind him or something? I'm sure he'd want to celebrate.'

'Maybe,' Aribella said. Theo was being kind, but she couldn't imagine Papa celebrating anything.

Theo seemed about to say something else when a sneering voice made them both turn.

'Well, well, well, look what the cat dragged in.'

Aribella's stomach dropped.

Gian was a tall boy, with greasy hair and lips that did not turn up at the edges when he smiled, though this did not often happen and was usually at someone else's expense.

Theo stiffened. 'Shove off, Gian.'

'Got every right to be here,' Gian replied. 'Not like her. She's not one of us.'

Theo's mouth opened to reply.

'Theo, it's fine,' Aribella said quickly. After years of this, she knew that Theo sticking up for her just made things worse. Gian looked for any excuse to have a fight. She'd learnt that the best reaction was no reaction at all.

Unfortunately, Gian seemed bored today. 'What's that you got there?' he asked, swiping the last half of Aribella's bread roll and shoving it in his mouth. 'Yuck, stale.' He spat the unchewed roll into the canal.

Aribella watched it disappear and tried not to think

12

of how hungry she would be later.

'You can't do that,' Theo said crossly. 'Here.'

He tried to hand Aribella the remains of his roll but she shook her head.

'It's fine, I'm not hungry.'

Gian was still looming over them, like a dark cloud. 'You heard what they're all saying at market? That blood moon stuff?'

Theo rolled his eyes. 'You're not listening to silly stories again, are you, Gian?'

'They're not silly stories! The blood moon is real. It's an omen.'

'An omen of what?' Theo scoffed.

Gian paused dramatically. 'That the dead are rising. Evil, soul-sucking spirits. Out on the lagoon.'

The hairs on Aribella's neck tingled as Gian's words hung in the air. Theo was silent. Did he believe this? she wondered – until she realized that he was struggling not to laugh. Her fear eased instantly as they both began to giggle.

Gian's face turned lobster red.

'If you believe that, then you're more stupid than you look,' Theo muttered, wiping the tears of laughter from his eyes, 'which is saying something.'

Gian's face went from red to purple. 'What did you say?' he barked, his eyes popping dangerously.

'Nothing,' Theo said innocently. 'Think Gian's hearing things, Ari.'

Aribella couldn't resist. 'Maybe it's the evil, soul-sucking spirits,' she murmured, and they both doubled over.

Gian's expression turned darker than a sea storm in winter. He grabbed Theo's shirt collar and pulled him to his feet.

'Let go of him!' Aribella shouted.

'You ought to be careful who you're loyal to, Theo,' Gian spat, ignoring her. 'She's not even from Burano. Nor her papa. No one knows where they came from but they don't belong with us.'

Theo twisted out of Gian's grip. 'Shut up!'

Gian's eyes gleamed malevolently. 'Why doesn't her papa leave his house? Why doesn't he talk to anyone? And what happened to her mama? She doesn't even know! Doesn't even know her own mama's name, I heard.'

Aribella tried not to react but her face was growing hot with shame. Who didn't know their own mama's name? Papa refused to tell her anything about Mama, however much she begged.

'Don't you dare talk about Aribella's family like that!' Theo snapped.

'Want to know what I think?' Gian asked, grinning.

'You *think*? That's a surprise,' Theo replied, squaring up to him.

'Theo, just leave it, please . . .' Aribella said.

'I think her papa killed her mama,' Gian went on. 'That's why he's so weird about it. That's why it's all a big secret.'

'That's not true!' Aribella shouted. She hated rising to Gian's bait but she couldn't stand him calling Papa a murderer. Papa had *loved* her mama, she was sure. This truth was what she held on to when she felt most lonely – that her parents had once loved each another. That Papa had once been happy. Sometimes it was all the comfort she had.

That was the moment her fingers began to tingle, quite suddenly, like pins and needles. At first she thought it was the cold – gutting fish all morning without gloves could do that – but it was such a strange sensation that she looked down at her hands. They were oddly blotchy. She clenched them into fists.

'My mama died too,' Theo growled. 'You want to tell me that my papa killed her?'

'Your mama died of pneumonia, everyone knows that. It wasn't some great big mystery.'

'Come on, Theo, let's get back to the stall,' Aribella urged. The tingling in her fingers was more painful now, like needles stabbing into her nail beds. What was going on? She stuffed her fists into her pockets and pushed past Gian, moving between the stalls. Theo followed.

'Yes, if you don't mind, we've got work to do,' he called back.

But Gian followed them to their table. 'Can't you see that I'm trying to help you, Theo? You'll catch something nasty hanging around with her.'

'Just so long as we don't catch stupidity from you,' Theo replied, loudly this time.

Gian's eyes flashed and pushed Theo hard, making him crash into a crate.

Aribella felt a rush of blood to her fingers, and a rush of something else – more urgent, angry and *hot* than anything she'd felt before. It coursed through her like a fever dream, like someone had lit a match and her whole body had become a firework about to rocket into the sky and explode. Her fingers were so full of the shooting pain now that tears sprang to her eyes. She saw Gian take another step towards Theo and, without thinking about it, her hands flew out of her pockets to grab Gian and pull him off, when –

Her fingers burst into flame.

It took Aribella a moment to comprehend what she was seeing. Her fingers were alight! Bright yellow sparks danced on each fingertip, as if her hands were made of matches. *What in the lagoon . . . ?*

She realized Gian was screaming. Panic seared through her. She released her grip and stumbled back, dazed. The sparks disappeared and Gian fell into another market stall with a crash, knocking eels all over the cobblestones. He continued to scream, writhing around in the eels, clutching his arm. His shirt, Aribella saw now, was frayed and burnt where her fingers had touched it. Did she really do that?

She stared down at her hands. The skin on her fingers was bright red and raw, as if she'd pressed them against a stove, and the pain was all too real.

Theo caught hold of her. 'Ari, are you all right? What did you . . . ?'

Aribella opened her mouth to explain but . . . how had she done it? She didn't understand.

'She burnt me,' Gian spluttered, finding his voice. Then he was stumbling to his feet, shouting, 'I knew she was bad, I knew it! *She's* the reason for the omens. She's a curse . . . a demon! A witch!'

'No!' Aribella gasped. It wasn't true. It couldn't be . . . Her entire body ached and stung, as if she'd swum a great distance, and she was horribly aware of the ominous hush that had fallen over the other market stalls and the countless faces that had turned to stare. Theo was standing beside her, but she couldn't bring

17

herself to look at his face. What would she see? Confusion, anger, fear? She couldn't bear it.

'Witch!' Gian screamed again. 'I'll put your name in the Lion's Mouth. You and your weird papa. Witch, witch, witch!'

Aribella couldn't move or speak. People were crowding round now. Other boys and girls took up Gian's chant: 'Witch, witch, witch!' Hands reached out to grab her.

'Get back,' someone shouted – maybe Theo – but Aribella was already twisting away from their grasps, already pelting from the market, her boots and heart pounding in unison. What had she done? How had that happened?

Aribella didn't dare look back. She raced across the Rialto, shoving through the crowds on the bridge, and plunged into the twisted and narrow streets on the other side of the city.

The ghastly chant carried on the wind behind her, following at every turn until she wasn't sure if it was real or in her head.

Witch, witch, witch . . .

But there was only so far she could run. Once her name was in the Lion's Mouth the guards would come looking . . . and what would she do then?

Aribella hid on the main island for the rest of the afternoon, lurking in shadowy alleyways and keeping out of sight. She eventually made her way to the *campanile* at Piazza San Marco, reasoning that any guards looking for her would not expect to find her so near the Doge's palace. How long did it take them to act on accusations from the Lion's Mouth?

She tried the tower door and found it unlocked. She climbed the hundreds of steps to the top and emerged into the open air. There, she sat under the enormous golden bell, looking down over the city she loved. The rooftops were so close it seemed as if they were whispering secrets to one another, as if they were one big family of which she was not a part.

Aribella shivered wretchedly and examined the new

scars on her fingers. Her mind reached for explanations but found none. How had this happened?

She sat there until her limbs ached. The bell bellowed above her every hour, sending nesting pigeons wheeling away and forcing Aribella to shove her sore hands over her ringing ears. In the last light of the setting sun, the bell rang five times, and she saw the silhouettes of the little fishing boats heading back towards Burano.

Gian must have put her name in the Lion's Mouth by now. Had he put Papa's name in too? Would the guards go to Burano tonight? Had they been already? She should have thought of that before. She briefly considered not returning to Burano at all – would that protect Papa? – but she had to at least warn him, if it wasn't already too late . . . What if she *was* too late? She should have left sooner.

Aribella stretched her aching limbs and hurriedly climbed back down to the square. Her stomach was growling like a wild animal. She kept her head down as she rushed towards the jetty where she managed to persuade a glass-blower from Murano to take her back to Burano in exchange for her lace-edged handkerchief. Mercifully, she asked few questions.

The sun dipped below the horizon as the boat crossed the lagoon, and the sky was dark by the time the glass-blower dropped her at Burano's harbour. Aribella ran through the cobbled streets, her pace only slowing when she reached the bridge that led to Via Fortuna. The name of their street had always struck her as ironic, given how little fortune they'd had. The only good fortune was that Theo lived there too.

The other cottages were quiet but their windows glowed, suggesting warm fires and hot dinners inside. She crept past, hoping no one would see her. She'd never felt more of an outsider in her life, as if she were a ghost haunting someone else's world.

She couldn't resist peering into Theo's kitchen window as she passed, but immediately regretted it. Inside, the table was laid and Theo's younger brother and sister were playing and laughing with their papa. Even without Theo, the happy scene filled Aribella with a longing as deep as an ocean. Theo's family might not have a mama any more either, but there was a warmth in their kitchen that she had never known in her own. Theo's house was a proper home.

His little sister Mia looked up and saw her. She smiled. Aribella's breath caught. She pressed a finger to her lips and slid back into the shadows, knowing that if Mia had been old enough to understand what had happened at the market today, she wouldn't have smiled like that. What about Theo? Did he hate her now? The thought was too awful.

Feeling utterly miserable, Aribella continued along the dark street, tensing at every noise – the hoot of an owl, the closing of a door. At last she reached Papa's bone-white cottage, which stood, bleak and cheerless, between the other more colourful cottages.

She paused. What if the guards were already inside? She listened carefully, but heard nothing.

A black shape shot out of the shadows making her jump.

'Oh, Luna, thank goodness it's only you!' Aribella whispered, her heart returning to its normal rhythm as she smiled down at the black cat tangling around her ankles. She scooped her up and buried her face in the warm fur.

Luna was the name Theo and Aribella had given the stray when they'd first found her on the harbour when they were small. They fed her scraps of fish left over from market and often saved her from the sting of Gian's boots. Aribella thought again about what had happened at the market, and quickly put Luna down. The cat mewed disgruntledly.

'I'm sorry, Luna. It's not safe. I might hurt you.' Aribella's lips quivered and her eyes filled with tears. She turned away and pushed through the front door into the tiny kitchen, blinking as her eyes adjusted to the gloom.

As usual, Papa hadn't lit any candles, so the only light came from a low fire in the hearth that needed stoking. The wind moaned through the chimney and sent the windows creaking like old bones. It was nearly as cold inside the kitchen as it was outside.

There was no sign of any guards. Papa was hunched in his rocking chair, a blanket wrapped round his frail shoulders.

His fingers flew back and forth across the trail of lace in his lap, like spiders weaving an intricate web. Even now, full of fear and panic, Aribella marvelled at his skill. The technique he used was called *punto in aria* – 'stitching in air'. But usually only women made lace; another reason Papa was so excluded.

The smell of cooked onions lingered, and Aribella noticed the black pot over the hearth. Papa must have made soup. She shut the door and stood wringing her blistered fingers, wondering where to begin.

'Papa, I've done something awful,' she said at last.

Papa looked up. His face creased into grooves of concern. It had been so long since he'd shown any signs of emotion that Aribella could hold on to herself no longer. Hot tears spilt down her cheeks.

'I did something, Papa, something I didn't mean to . . . something I don't even know how to explain.'

She knew she wasn't making any sense. But how could she get Papa to understand when she didn't understand it herself?

'I was angry,' she began, looking at the floor instead of at him. 'This boy was saying nasty things at the market. About Mama. Theo tried to stick up for me but the boy attacked him, and then I don't know what happened, I was just so angry I . . . I sort of exploded. There was this rushing feeling – all the way through me.' Aribella tried to remember exactly what had happened. 'Then my fingers were stinging, and suddenly sparks shot out of them . . . little flames of fire. I know it sounds mad but I swear I'm not lying! And now Gian – the boy – he's going to put my name in the Lion's Mouth, Papa, and maybe yours too. They could come for us at any moment. I'm so sorry. I can't believe I did this. I don't know how I did this or what any of it means. It feels like an awful dream, like a nightmare . . .'

She could barely breathe, her chest was so tight. But there it was, the truth – at least, what she understood of it – out in the open between her and Papa. But what of the part she didn't understand? Was she really a curse? A witch?

She looked up. Papa's face had gone quite white and his eyes had grown wide.

'Did anyone else see it happen?'

Aribella was not sure what startled her more, the rare sound of Papa's voice, his sudden urgency, or the fact that he seemed to believe her. Shouldn't he protest more, say it couldn't be true? Instead, he seemed both afraid and strangely unsurprised. As if, somehow, he'd been expecting this.

She nodded shamefully. 'It was at the market. I'm not sure how many people saw but Gian will have told them all anyway. I'm so sorry, Papa. I've put you in danger and I don't even understand how it happened. We have to leave Venice. Right now.'

Papa sat back in his chair and rubbed his forehead wearily. 'And go where?'

'I don't know,' Aribella admitted. They had no money, no boat, no family or friends who might help. And Papa was so frail.

'We can't run away, Bella,' Papa said softly.

There was resignation in his voice. She wished he'd hug her and tell her everything was going to be all right, but he stayed in his chair, staring into the fire, already a million miles away.

'Have some soup,' he said eventually.

'I'm not hungry.' But her stomach growled traitorously.

'Have some soup.' It wasn't a suggestion.

Aribella went to the pot and ladled onion soup into a bowl. She didn't bother with a spoon, just put the bowl to her lips and drank. The soup was lukewarm and bland, but it eased the empty feeling inside her. She swayed on the spot and realized her eyelids were drooping. Her entire body was still aching.

'Bed now, Bella.'

'But, Papa!' How could she possibly sleep at a time like this? 'What if—'

'Bed – *now*.' Papa's voice was suddenly hard as a slammed door. His tone shocked her. But she did as he said. What else could she do?

Aribella climbed the rickety staircase up to her bedroom with a heavy heart, clutching at the small hope that if the guards weren't here yet, then maybe Gian hadn't put her name in the Mouth. Maybe Theo had stopped him, or the Doge hadn't believed it . . . Even so, these thoughts did little to comfort her. All she could think about were the flames in her fingers, and what they might mean for her and for those she loved. If she was a witch or a curse, she shouldn't be on Burano near Theo or Papa, or anyone at all.

4

'Bedroom' had always been a generous term for the pokey room where Aribella's thin, lumpy mattress curled up the walls. It was a good thing she didn't have more than two changes of clothes, for there would be nowhere to put them and the low rafters meant she always had to stoop. The room was unbearably hot and sticky in the summer and freezing in the winter.

She removed her boots but lay down on her mattress fully dressed, knowing she would not sleep. Endless questions tumbled through her head. What would she do if the guards came? Even if she and Papa had money, where could they go? Venice had always been her home and she dearly loved the floating city and its islands. She knew so little of her mama, but she had lived and died in Venice and being here gave Aribella a feeling of connection to her. Perhaps that was why Papa didn't want to leave either. But why hadn't he seemed more surprised by what had happened?

She regarded her fingers warily in the moonshine that spilt through the window. But no, that couldn't be moonshine, the colour was so strange. Aribella looked up, confused, and crawled to her window.

The moon was full and low – and red.

A jolt of shock passed through her. *The blood moon's real. It's an omen . . .* Could it be? Had the fisherman and Gian been right? She leapt to her feet and banged her head on the rafters, falling back to her knees.

'Ow!' she groaned, then shut up immediately.

There were footsteps marching in the street below, men with heavy boots – *guards*. It had to be. Fear clenched round Aribella's heart.

BOOM, BOOM, BOOM!

Fists thundered on the front door of their cottage.

'Open up!'

She could hear Papa shuffling around downstairs. *No, Papa, don't let them in!*

'Open up!' came the voice again, and then there was the sound of wood splintering. They were breaking the door down! She heard more shouting, then Papa cried out. She had to help!

And now came another sound, right behind her. Someone was coming in through her window! Aribella scrambled to her feet and flew towards the door. A hand grabbed her arm, and another clamped over her mouth. Aribella gasped for breath, tearing desperately at the hands.

'Shh, Ari. It's me.'

'Theo?' She stopped struggling.

'I saw the guards coming,' he said hurriedly, pulling her to the window. 'We have to get you out of here.'

Downstairs, glasses smashed. There was more shouting.

'I need to help Papa!' she whispered.

'You can't,' Theo replied frantically. 'They'll be up here for you soon. Come on.'

Aribella could hear the neighbours calling to each other in the street, wondering what the commotion in the white house was about.

'The moon!' she heard one of them shout. 'The omen!'

Heavy footsteps stomped up the stairs. Aribella had seconds left to decide, but she knew Theo was right. They clambered out of the window and on to the roof just in time.

BANG. The door of her room slammed open.

Aribella and Theo scrambled further away from the window. The roof tiles slipped precariously underneath them. They grabbed hold of the chimney and crouched behind it, clutching each other, bathed in the strange light from the moon. The wind was cold and wild around them as if it were trying to capture them too.

She heard footsteps cross her bedroom floor, moving towards the window.

For a few terrifying seconds they held their breath, hidden behind the chimney. The seconds seemed to stretch for eternity. Aribella's heart was beating so loudly she was sure the guard would hear it.

Finally they heard him shout, 'She's not here!'

As his footsteps retreated, Aribella gulped air. But her relief was short-lived.

'Two of you take the old man back to the palace prison,' the guard called. 'The rest of you search the island. She can't have got far.'

Aribella and Theo stayed on the roof, shivering, as the guards spread out across Burano. They banged on doors, searched homes, questioned nightgowned fishermen. Aribella's heart broke as she watched two guards lead poor Papa away. Theo had to restrain her a second time from climbing down and chasing after them.

At last the guards' lanterns moved towards the harbour, before disappearing against the inky darkness of the lagoon.

Only then did Theo release his grip on her arm.

'I should have stopped them taking Papa,' Aribella sobbed. 'I should have made them take me instead.'

Theo shook his head. 'You couldn't save him, Ari. Gian put both your names in the Lion's Mouth. And if you're caught, what use would you be to your papa?'

'What use can I be to him now?'

'You can go to see the Doge. Try to explain. He's a kind man, I'm sure he'll—'

'What? Understand?' Aribella snapped. She hated her bitter tone but it all felt so hopeless. How could she possibly explain to the Doge what she didn't understand herself? She sighed. 'Sorry, Theo.'

'It's all right.'

'It's not. Thanks for coming to help.' She looked up again at the ominous red moon, and shuddered.

'The moon, Theo . . . It's the blood moon. Gian was right.'

Theo looked up and chewed his lip. 'Guess there's a first time for everything.'

Aribella didn't smile. 'You should get away, Theo,' she whispered. 'You're too kind to me and it's dangerous for you.'

'Rubbish, Ari.'

'But what if I am a curse? Was Gian right about that too?'

'Look, so what if the moon is red?' Theo said. 'Do you honestly believe it's an omen of the dead rising?'

Aribella shook her head. 'I don't know . . .' She didn't know what to believe any more. She turned away from Theo and crawled back across the roof, sliding in through the window.

Her room looked the same as she had left it, but downstairs was another matter. The door was hanging off its hinges, splintered and broken. The fire had been trodden out and the few possessions Papa owned were scattered everywhere, mostly smashed to pieces – bowls, plates, glasses . . . His beautiful lace had been torn to shreds. Aribella sank to her knees.

A meow came from the doorway.

'Luna!' The cat jumped into her arms, and buried her face in Aribella's chest, as if she knew how much Aribella's heart was hurting. It helped, just a little.

'Oh, Ari, I'm so sorry,' Theo murmured.

Aribella found she couldn't speak. She pressed Luna closer to her.

'You can tell me, you know, Ari.' Theo said it so softly that Aribella almost didn't hear. 'About earlier . . . at the market. You can trust me.'

'I know.' If there was anyone in the world she could trust, it was Theo. But what could she tell him? She might be putting him in danger too.

Before she could say anything else, Luna tensed, jumped out of Aribella's arms and ran outside.

'Luna, come back!'

Aribella hurried after the black cat – and froze. At the end of Via Fortuna, a cloaked figure stood on the bridge. He was wearing a mask. Aribella shot back into the house.

'Theo! There's still a guard here. What do we do?'

'Did he see you?'

'I don't know . . .'

'My boat,' Theo said at once, as if he'd been concocting this plan the whole time. 'We'll row out around the island until he's gone. Quick – back to the roof.'

5

Moving as fast as they dared without making too much noise, Aribella and Theo raced upstairs to her room, where Aribella quickly shoved on her boots. Then they clambered out of the window and across the roof again, using the windowsills to climb down the back of the house, before pelting to the harbour, where Theo's boat was tied.

Between the local fishing boats one unfamiliar craft was moored – a black gondola. It was utterly out of place, like a stallion amid ponies. Aribella looked at it with fear, and Theo, she was sure, with admiration. She noticed a golden winged lion painted on the gondola's hull – the symbol of Venice.

Theo had been given his boat for his thirteenth birthday, a hand-me-down from a fisherman whose son had outgrown it. It was full of patched leaks and its paint peeled like old fish scales, but it was his pride and joy.

Theo unlooped the mooring rope as Aribella jumped aboard, then climbed in himself. The boat rocked under both their weights, and Aribella held on tightly as Theo began to row away from Burano's safe harbour.

The cold wind cut through their clothes. Aribella was glad of her thick woollen jumper, but the freezing water in the bottom of the boat went through the holes in her boots. They had no lantern to give them away, and pulled quietly out into the darkness with nothing but the red moon to guide them. Even the stars seemed to be hiding tonight. A thick white mist lay further out on the lagoon.

She heard a flapping noise overhead, like leather gloves slapping together, and looked up to see a small dark shape flitting back and forth against the red moon. Just a bat. Nothing unusual, but she shivered as she looked down at the trembling black water.

'Theo, do you remember what Gian said about the blood moon and the lagoon?'

'Ari, since when have you listened to Gian? The moon may be red but no evil soul-sucking spirits are coming to get us. The only thing we have to worry

35

about is that guard. We'll stay out here for a little longer and then he's bound to get bored. If he comes looking this way, we'll spot him a mile off. All right?'

The stretch of black sea between them and Burano was empty, and the white mist lay in front of them. Maybe Theo was right. She let out a shuddering breath she didn't realize she'd been holding, and tried to relax. It *was* just a silly story. Evil spirits didn't rise out of lagoons. But then fire wasn't meant to come out of your fingers either . . .

'Theo . . .'

Behind him, a light was flickering and bobbing in the darkness. A gondola's lantern. The masked guard! How had he got so close without them seeing him?

'Theo, row!' she hissed.

'What?'

'I think it's the guard!'

Theo started to row faster, pulling the oars as quickly as he could. But Aribella could see the shape of an elegant gondola now, and it was slipping through the water like silk, gaining on them.

Aribella looked around desperately. The mist that lay on the lagoon was even closer.

Theo was smiling bravely. 'What luck! We're bound to lose him in this.'

'What if we get lost ourselves?' Aribella asked nervously. But the gondola was fast approaching. They had no other option.

The mist loomed over them and then they were inside its damp whiteness. Aribella could no longer see the gondola or the blood moon. She could barely see Theo at the other end of the boat.

'*Santa cielo*, this is thick!' Theo sounded as if he were at the end of a long tunnel.

A sudden wave sent the boat spinning in disorientating circles. Aribella gripped the sides, her stomach lurching. She heard a horrible clunk, and Theo groaned.

'Oh no! I've lost one of the oars.' He sounded desperate. 'I'm so sorry, Ari.'

'It's all right, don't worry,' she tried to reassure him, but they were not going to get far with only one oar. They were on a fishing boat, not a gondola. The mist was everywhere, blotting out everything, more waves rocked the boat, and soon they had swung in so many circles that Aribella was no longer sure where Burano was. She tried to quell her rising panic.

Aribella wasn't afraid of water when it was calm and glassy – it would be hard to get about in Venice if that were the case, given canals were roads and homes were on islands – but she *was* afraid of water when it was stormy, when it became uncontrolled and wild and could wreck ships and steal lives.

There had been a storm the night Mama died, that was all Papa had told her. He said she'd drowned on the lagoon but had never explained what Mama was doing out there. Why had she been out on a boat at night alone? Had she got lost in mist just like this?

Aribella hadn't meant to think of Mama, but she surfaced in her mind now, shadowy and enigmatic, more idea than solid shape. Aribella could only recall the smell of her hair, the softness of her arms.

Theo tried rowing again but it was useless with only one oar. Aribella tried to keep her breathing steady as she strained to see into the gloom, searching for familiar landforms. They must be north of Burano now, on the open lagoon, heading . . . east?

Suddenly, a patch of the mist cleared and the red moon illuminated the dark outline of an island. Aribella's heart leapt – land! Thank goodness! But she soon realized it was not any island she knew. In the centre of it was a large hill, on top of which was a crumbling palazzo. The mist separated the island from the water so that it appeared to be floating.

The hairs on the back of Aribella's neck stood up. But the next moment the mist veil fell once again and the island was swallowed up. Aribella blinked, breathing quickly.

She was about to tell Theo about it when a sharp hiss cut through the muffled silence, like a fast-moving wind through trees. But there were no trees, just mist and sea . . . She looked back the way they had come, searching for the source of the sound. The mist seemed to press into her ears and eyes, blinding and deafening her.

From behind Theo, louder and clearer, came another sound – a slithering, like an oar moving through water, or a sea snake. Aribella whipped her head round. Something pale was emerging out of the mist behind the boat, behind Theo. Something so strange and so terrifying that it looked as if it had come right out of a nightmare, with two dark eye sockets and a face that gleamed, white as bone . . . A human skull floated in the mist, detached from everything.

The dead had risen, just as Gian had said.

Aribella heard her own scream rip through the air before she was aware she'd let it out.

'Ari? What is it?' Theo twisted this way and that, looking in every direction, before turning back to her. 'Are you all right?'

He could neither see it nor hear it, she realized, with fresh dread. But why?

The skull moved closer to Theo, its dark jaws unhinged, and made another horrible hiss that chilled

Aribella to her core.

'Theo!' she screamed.

Theo leapt to his feet and the boat see-sawed under his weight. Aribella scrambled for the oar and lifted it just as the skull fixed its jaws round Theo's cheek.

Theo staggered backwards, crying out. Though he could not see the skull, he could definitely feel it.

Aribella swung at the skull with all her might, but it dissolved back into the mist and the oar smacked into the side of Theo's head instead. A horrible crack echoed into the night. Theo dropped like a stone into the belly of the boat.

6

'No!' Aribella threw down the oar and scrambled to Theo's side.

His eyes were closed and he wasn't moving.

Please don't be dead . . .

She heard the skull hiss again, this time from above her. The fear was like cold water dripping down her spine, but now it turned to fury. Urgent, angry and *hot*.

Tremors ripped through her whole body, becoming sharp pains as they coursed into her fingers. Her hands were shaking.

It was happening again! She moved away from Theo and cried out in agony as the barely healed skin on each of her fingertips ignited. Bright, yellow sparks ripped out and lit up the darkness, stronger than before. Some instinct took over and she raised her burning hands above her head, directing the flames towards the skull. The pain in her fingers was unbearable. Stars exploded in her head and her vision swam with black spots.

Still, she held on.

The skull shrieked and hissed, wheeling away into the mist. The reflections of the flames danced upon the surface of the lagoon, making Aribella feel as though the whole world was water and fire. The skull wheeled higher and higher, still making that horrible hissing, until the mist swallowed it completely.

Panting, Aribella clenched her fists and the sparks went out.

'Theo . . .' She stumbled back towards him but her foot caught on the oar and she fell. The boat rocked wildly then completely overturned, tumbling both her and Theo into the lagoon.

Shock jolted through Aribella's body as she plunged underwater. Her fingers went from burning to freezing. She breathed in water and choked, her chest tightening as she sank. Her arms were like lead and her lungs were squeezing shut, but she could not give up. Theo needed her. She kicked upwards desperately, her muscles almost spent. The surface was still so far away . . . but now there were glittering stars to draw her. Just when she thought she was done for, strong hands grabbed her wrists and pulled her up.

Aribella came spluttering to the surface and was hauled over the side of a boat. She collapsed in a dripping heap. Her wet clothes clung to her body and her hair stuck to her forehead. The mist was gone, the moon was silver again and the stars were out, but as Aribella gulped the fresh, cold air, she realized the glittering stars that had drawn her to the surface were sequinned stars on the face of a black velvet mask, sewn with artistry beyond even Papa's skills.

Aribella had a funny feeling, as she looked from the mask to the night sky, that the pattern of sequins exactly matched the arrangement of the *real* stars. And for a moment, she was so taken by this thought and the mask's beauty that she almost forgot what it meant. But her wonder quickly turned to dread as she registered she was lying in the bottom of a black gondola. The guard had caught them after all.

Behind his starry mask, the man's eyes shone, and he wore an indigo cloak that, like his mask, was decorated with stars. His bald head was covered in tattoos.

At the other end of the gondola, she heard a groan. Theo lay there, his eyes closed.

'Theo!' She clambered towards him, wincing at the yellow bruise on his temple which she'd caused with the oar. But there was a far worse mark staining the other side of Theo's freckled face: a pattern of black veins that spread from his face and down his neck where the skull had bitten him. It was as if his skin was infected by some terrible disease.

'Theo!' She shook him as violently as she dared. He was barely breathing. 'Oh, Theo, please wake up!'

'What happened?' the guard asked.

'You won't believe me.'

'Try me.' There was a touch of playfulness in his tone.

Aribella gave him a sideways glare. 'This thing, this skull, it came out of the mist—'

'A spectre?' His tone was deadly serious now.

Aribella started. The guard hadn't questioned what'd she'd said at all. In fact, he spoke as though he knew of this *spectre*. 'I don't know, Theo couldn't see it, but that mark on his face is where it bit him. I think it's done something terrible to him and that's why he won't wake up. We need help.'

The guard was already rummaging in his cloak. From an inside pocket, he withdrew a small vial of golden liquid which glowed in the darkness.

Aribella bristled. 'What's that?'

'Something that will help. Pour a few drops on the wound . . . Do it quickly. I know you have questions but there isn't time to explain. You have to trust me.'

'Why should I?' After all, hadn't he just chased them out here? He was going to take her to prison with Papa . . .

'Firstly, because I'm telling the truth. Secondly, because you want to save your friend and this is the only thing that will work. And thirdly, because you don't have a choice.'

He was right – what was the alternative? The mark had already spread to Theo's shoulder.

Reluctantly, Aribella took the vial, removed the stopper and let a few golden drops fall on to Theo's cheek. As they were absorbed into Theo's skin the black veins began to fade, and soon he looked as if he was just sleeping peacefully. When he let out a juddering breath, Aribella almost wept with relief.

'What is this stuff?' she asked, holding up the vial.

'Four Thieves Vinegar. The only antidote to spectre bites. I don't have anything to help with the pain in your fingers, I'm afraid. It always hurts using that much power without a mask.'

Aribella understood nothing of what this man said. Why would wearing a mask make any difference? And how did he know about the pain in her fingers anyway? Her mind whirled. If the guard was here to arrest her, he was doing it in a very odd manner.

She tucked the vial in her trouser pocket and tried to

45

focus. She'd deal with the guard and whatever he had in store for her later. First, she had to persuade him to get Theo to safety.

'Please, you must take my friend back to Burano. He's done nothing wrong. He's soaked and needs to get warm. Then you can do what you want with me. Imprison me or hang me . . .' Her voice got so thick that it stuck in her throat and she had to swallow several times.

For a moment, the guard did not reply. Then he did something entirely unexpected – he threw back his head and laughed. The sound was light and bright.

Aribella glared at him. How dare he laugh at a time like this? What had happened to her life might be a laughing matter to him, but it certainly was not to her.

'Forgive me. My dear girl, I can assure you I've no plans to imprison or hang you. Unless, of course, you continue to drip on my favourite cushion.'

Aribella looked down. She hadn't even noticed the fine cushion she was crouching on. She stood, wondering if this man was crazy, and tried to keep her body between him and Theo.

'What do you want then?' she asked, trying to sound braver than she felt.

'To introduce myself.' The guard untied the velvet ribbons of his mask and removed it. Underneath, his

46

features were fox-like. He had more wrinkles criss-crossing his cheeks and forehead than Papa, and his skin was wind-worn, like a fisherman's. His beard was grey and pointed, and now she could see that the tattoos which covered his bald head were a strange pattern of waxing and waning moons.

The man bowed. 'Rodolfo Foscari. Delighted to meet you, Aribella.'

'You know my name . . . You got it from the Lion's Mouth, didn't you?'

'I did. But you should not be afraid.'

'Of course I should be afraid! The other guards took Papa away!'

Rodolfo frowned and his wrinkles deepened. 'I'm sorry to hear that but I'm sure there's something we can do to help your papa.'

Aribella regarded him warily. 'You're lying. The Doge sent you to capture us because I'm—' She stopped.

Rodolfo's eyebrows rose. 'Because you're what?'

She swallowed and looked down at her soggy boots. The words came out of her mouth before she could stop them. 'Because I'm strange.'

When she looked up, Rodolfo was smiling. 'Do you want to know the secret about being a misfit? You're never the only one. You just haven't found where you

47

belong yet. You are no stranger than me, than the rest of us. You are a Cannovacci, Aribella.'

'A *what?*'

'A person with powers. I'm one too. A star-reader.' He held up the starry mask.

'A star-reader? What does that mean?'

'It's rather complicated and this must be overwhelming. Don't worry, everything will be explained in due course. First, however, we need to get your friend home. I'm assuming he hasn't got any hidden talents?'

Theo gave a loud snore and murmured, 'Pretty boat, my boat . . . boat.'

Theo's boat! Aribella looked around. It must have sunk to the bottom of the lagoon. Her stomach twisted with guilt. Theo had loved that boat more than anything in the world and his papa would never be able to afford to replace it, especially now there were so few fish to catch.

Rodolfo put his star mask back on and slid the gondola's long, single oar back into the oarlock. The gondola turned in an elegant circle. If they'd been able to do that in Theo's boat, they might have got away from that awful spectre . . . *The rising dead* . . . She shivered and pushed the thought away, only to have it replaced by another: *a Cannovacci . . . a person with powers*

. . . What did that mean?

The movement of the gondola was swan-like and serene, a world away from the clunky motion of Theo's boat. Soon they were flying across the lagoon, gathering so much speed that Aribella's knotted black hair flapped behind her and her breath was snatched from her throat. Goosebumps rippled across her skin. The wind was icy but exhilarating, and even in her state of turmoil, Aribella felt thrilled at the speed of the air rushing by. She'd thought gondolas were fast but this was something else. How was it possible to move so quickly? She wished Theo had been awake to experience it.

In hardly any time at all the familiar shape of Burano appeared ahead of them. The little cottages looked fragile against the darkness now that Aribella knew awful creatures like the spectre were lurking on the lagoon.

Rodolfo slid the gondola up to a mooring post. Aribella climbed out, shivering.

'Here, put this on.' Rodolfo unbuckled the clasp round his neck and held out his star cloak. 'You're going to need it on the way back.'

Way back to where? Reluctantly, Aribella took the cloak and put it round her shoulders. It was much too long and heavy so she had to be careful not to trip, but it was surprisingly warm and soft and a welcome relief from her damp clothes.

Rodolfo lifted Theo over one shoulder. 'Lead the way!'

She took him down the empty streets to Via Fortuna and Theo's cottage, wondering what people would think if they looked out of their windows. But no faces appeared, and they reached Theo's cottage unnoticed.

Rodolfo laid Theo on the cobblestones outside his door. Warm light spilt out from the kitchen window and over Theo's face. The yellow bruise remained on his temple, but the black mark was almost gone. Only a dim circle remained under his skin, like a shadow.

Theo's eyelids fluttered. 'Ari,' he murmured.

'We should go,' Rodolfo said.

'Can't I say goodbye?' Aribella pleaded. She didn't want to leave Theo without an explanation.

'It's best he wakes up alone. The healing of the Four Thieves Vinegar is deep. The last few hours will vanish like a dream and he'll be better off without those memories. Don't worry, you'll see him soon.'

Aribella was not sure she believed this, but she wanted to protect Theo. Rodolfo gave Theo's front door two sharp raps then retreated, gesturing for Aribella to follow. With an aching heart, Aribella joined him in the shadows. They were still in plain view of the doorway.

'But won't they see us here?' she asked.

'Oh, don't worry about that.' Rodolfo tapped his starry mask. 'My mask makes us unwatchable when necessary.'

'Makes us *what*?'

'*Unwatchable*,' Rodolfo replied, a little impatiently. 'But not *unhearable*, so please shush.'

Aribella fought down the questions that leapt to her tongue as Theo's door swung open and warm light poured into the street. Relieved exclamations from Theo's papa, brothers and sister carried into the night air. Aribella wanted to cry out to them, to run into their arms too, but their hugs weren't meant for her. So she remained silent beside Rodolfo. No one seemed to see them, as he had said.

The last thing she heard before they took him inside was Theo exclaiming, 'Papa, what's going on? How did I get here?' Then the door closed and the street was dark once more.

Goodbye, Theo. Aribella's stomach twisted. Would she ever see him again?

'Come on,' Rodolfo said. 'If you want to help your papa, we should get back to the Halfway Hotel and tell the others what has happened here.' He turned back towards the harbour.

The Halfway Hotel? Was that some cruel nickname for the prison? And what others?

It could still be a trick, but Rodolfo had completed his part of the bargain and taken Theo home. Taking a deep breath, Aribella turned away from Burano, from everything she knew, and followed Rodolfo.

Her heart was full of worries for her papa, fear for what her future might hold and sadness that she hadn't said goodbye to Theo. But underneath was the strangest flutter of excitement, like a tiny bird flexing its wings, growing stronger with every step towards the harbour. She felt as if she had been waiting her whole life for something to happen, something that would show her who she was – and this, bizarrely enough, felt like it might be it.

Indeed, something about stepping back into the gondola felt like the start of an adventure.

The gondola moved so smoothly away from the harbour that it took Aribella a moment to realize Rodolfo had started rowing. As it gathered speed once more, the *ferro* dipped like the neck of a racehorse. The wind whipped back Aribella's hair and sent the borrowed star cloak flapping about her shoulders. It was as if they weren't even on the surface of the water any more, but gliding through the air.

They soon left Burano far behind. All around was nothing but water, the shadows of distant islands, the moon and stars. The lagoon was beautiful and glassy, full of silver reflections. It was magical and peaceful, and hard to believe that this was the same lagoon on which the horrid skull had appeared less than an hour ago. The night sky was clear and mist-free, and the stars looked so close and crisp that Aribella felt she could reach out and pluck one right out of the sky and wear it as a jewel. There were no other boats out and the beauty of the lagoon seemed to exist for Aribella's eyes alone.

From behind her came the first notes of a tune, and Aribella turned to look. Rodolfo's tall and wiry frame was silhouetted against the moon, and he was singing one of the folk songs of the gondoliers, she realized, recognizing it. She and Theo had heard them haunting the lagoon their whole lives. The sound always unlocked something deep inside Aribella, something she didn't fully understand. Rodolfo's singing seemed to echo further across the lagoon than seemed possible, almost as if he were sending a message, and it soothed her frayed nerves.

Soon, the main island appeared, its domes and spires duplicated upon the surface of the lagoon, so that it seemed as if there were two cities – a city of the water and a city of the air – shimmering with dual possibilities. Aribella had never seen the main island at this time of night before; it was strange and ghostly without the usual daytime crowds. The gondolas outside the palace were motionless at their posts and a brooding stillness settled over everything. A spike of fear returned to Aribella's heart as she looked at the winged chimeras, angels and gargoyles engraved in the palace walls, at the Lion's Mouth and the palace prison . . . Was Papa already there? Her imagination filled with subterranean chambers and torture devices. Few knew what the palace prison was like inside, as those that crossed the famous Bridge of Sighs rarely returned.

Rodolfo must have caught the direction of her gaze. 'Don't worry,' he called, 'we'll help your papa. But there's somewhere else we need to go first.'

He swung the gondola into the Grand Canal. The boat began to rock for the first time, not clumsily like Theo's boat but as if it was rearing, and Aribella again had the strange sense that it was alive.

'She doesn't like the canals as much as the open water,' said Rodolfo. 'They make her feel trapped. I understand how she feels sometimes.'

Another bizarre statement, but with everything else going on Aribella didn't question it. Especially since a small black bat had just flown out of the darkness and landed on Rodolfo's shoulder. It folded its leathery wings and looked at her, its beady eyes shining in the lantern light. Aribella wasn't sure how to recognize one bat from another, but she was somehow sure this was the same bat she had seen on the lagoon.

'Aribella, this is Io,' announced Rodolfo.

'That bat is your pet?'

'Companion,' Rodolfo corrected her. 'I'm more his pet than he is mine – hold on!' he added as the gondola rocked again.

They continued to move down the Grand Canal, taking the route Aribella and Theo always took to the *pescheria*, heading towards the heart of the floating city. But when they reached the Rialto Bridge, the gondola slowed and, instead of passing underneath, to Aribella's astonishment, they slid up to the jetty of the dilapidated palazzo she'd always loved.

'We're here!' Rodolfo announced cheerily.

The yellow paint was still peeling, the windows were dark and empty, and the ancient jetty had several boards missing. Was this supposed to be the Halfway Hotel? Surely, Rodolfo had made a mistake.

'I'll just tie her up. You can go on inside.'

He fastened the gondola to one of the splintered mooring posts and ushered her on to the broken jetty. Aribella had to be careful where she put her feet so she didn't go right through the boards. Rodolfo's expression was hidden behind his star mask but she wondered if he was teasing her. She was cold and tired and not in the mood for jokes.

Feeling unsure, she waited while Rodolfo knelt and stroked the gondola. It hummed in a way that reminded Aribella of purring but must surely be vibrations from the water. All of a sudden, the gondola began to sink into the canal.

'Signore, your boat!' she cried out.

'It's perfectly fine, don't worry. She's off to bed. Well, go on in!' Rodolfo urged, nodding towards the entrance.

Aribella had no idea what was going on, or why Rodolfo was so unconcerned that his beautiful gondola had just sunk to the bottom of the canal. She turned to the palazzo. What if he'd been lying and the Doge's guards were waiting for her? But then why wouldn't he just have taken her to the prison?

She didn't know where the doors of the palazzo would lead her but she knew she had to go through. If there was even the smallest chance that by stepping inside she would find out why so many strange things were happening to her, then she had to do it.

Taking a deep breath, Aribella picked her way across the missing boards to the doors. The orange-and-purple stained glass must have been beautiful once but now it was so smashed you could hardly tell.

Gingerly, Aribella pushed open the doors and peered inside. The lobby must also have been grand once but now it was just as dark and neglected as the exterior. The stone floor was cracked from flooding in the high tides of the *acqua alta*, and the soot-blackened fireplace looked as if it hadn't been used for centuries. The sweeping staircase had too many stairs missing to be useable, and the sagging ceiling beams looked as though they might collapse at any moment. Pigeons had made an untidy nest in the corners of the room and a mournful coo echoed through the empty chamber, along with the dripping sound of a leak. The smell of mould clogged her nose and she could hear the scuttling of rats.

'You've got to go all the way in or else you won't see,' Rodolfo called from behind her.

Aribella gritted her teeth and resisted the urge to tell him he was crazy. The palazzo was obviously abandoned. But as soon as both of her feet crossed the threshold, everything changed. Aribella blinked in amazement.

The pigeon nests disappeared, the walls covered themselves with plum-coloured wallpaper, and a soft orange carpet unfurled beneath her damp feet. Gleaming mahogany coffee tables appeared – complete with soft lampshades and vases of sweet-smelling peonies. Sofas materialized out of the air, piled with plump cushions. The previously empty fireplace filled with a roaring fire. Candlesticks flew through the air to land neatly at either end of the newly fixed mantelpiece.

The staircase repaired itself and a huge reception desk sprang up in front of it.

Aribella stepped back out on to the broken jetty in alarm, only the jetty wasn't broken any more either! It looked freshly polished and good as new. The mooring posts were no longer splintered and rotten, but striped like candy cane with gleaming golden rings.

Aribella's jaw dropped further as she gazed up at the palazzo's facade – the canary-yellow paint was no longer dull and peeling but bright and cheerful, and the windows that had been dark and empty now glowed with warm candlelight. Stained-glass diamonds on the entrance door sparkled merrily in the light of lanterns on either side. The door handles had reshaped themselves into golden winged lions, like the one painted on Rodolfo's boat. And in swirling letters above the doorway, a sign read: *Welcome to the Halfway Hotel.*

'But . . . how . . . ?' Aribella exclaimed, struggling to speak.

Rodolfo laughed again, as he had done on the lagoon, light and bright. He held up three fingers and counted them off one by one. 'Never judge a book by its cover. Never judge a person by their mask. And never judge a hotel by her facade. Most people are so preoccupied with how things appear on the surface that they never find out what they're really like. The

Halfway only shows her beauty to the Cannovacci who step over the threshold.'

Aribella continued to gaze up at the hotel in wonder. She'd always loved the palazzo but now it was easily the most beautiful building on the Grand Canal. Theo would not tease her for liking it if he could see this . . . Her chest tightened at the thought of him.

'This . . . *this* is the Halfway Hotel?'

'What were you expecting?'

Something more like the palace prison. 'Why is it called the Halfway Hotel?' she asked, reaching for anything she could make sense of.

'Because it's halfway along the Grand Canal, of course,' Rodolfo said. 'Come on.' He held the door open for her. Io flew off his shoulders and into the lobby.

Aribella followed the bat, allowing herself a tiny flutter of pleasure at the thought of how furious Gian would be if he knew just where his note in the Lion's Mouth had got her.

8

Now that she was no longer in a state of *complete* shock, Aribella could see that the new lobby was both cosy and elegant, and she loved it. The large reception desk in front of the staircase now had a vase of white roses at either end and rows of golden keys on hooks behind it.

A lady stood behind the desk, her silver-grey hair immaculately coiffed in a bun. She was wearing bright red lipstick and a matching crimson evening gown. She looked very glamorous and Aribella was suddenly acutely aware of her scruffy, damp clothes and the squelch of her boots. The familiar feeling of being out of place tugged at her, and she chewed her lip.

But the lady smiled warmly. '*Buona sera!*' she called.

Io landed on the reception desk and the lady gave

him a little stroke behind one ear.

'*Buona sera*, Rosa!' Rodolfo removed his star mask and bowed. 'Aribella, meet Rosa, the Halfway Hotel's key keeper.'

'I got your message,' Rosa replied. 'This must be our new guest. Welcome, Aribella.'

When had Rodolfo sent a message? Aribella wondered. But then she remembered Rodolfo singing, and her strange sense that it could travel further than seemed possible . . . Had the song been a secret message? The thought made her head spin even more than the lobby's transformation.

'What a frightening experience you've had tonight. Poor petal,' Rosa said kindly.

Aribella was not used to kindness, especially from glamorous ladies like Rosa. She smiled back shyly and shuffled her feet.

'I'm sorry we couldn't get to you before your father was taken. But we haven't found a new Cannovacci through the Lion's Mouth for years. It was quite exciting, wasn't it, Nymeria?'

Something moved near the foot of the staircase, half hidden by the desk – an enormous golden creature, which yawned and shook out its mane. It was a lion, Aribella realized, an actual lion! Just like the ones on the door handles and the gondola, except for the

62

wings. She'd never seen a lion in real life before.

Rodolfo went over and tickled Nymeria behind the ear, as if the beast was nothing but a house cat. 'No need to be alarmed, Aribella. Nymeria is here to warn us if Venice should ever be in danger. But she is a gentle soul. Unless you get on her wrong side, of course, much like Rosa here.'

'Careful, Rodolfo.' Rosa tutted but her eyes shone.

'See what I mean?' Rodolfo winked.

Aribella was still trying to make sense of it all. This hotel had been ruined and now it was beautiful, and there was a key keeper who kept an actual lion as a pet – or *companion* or whatever it was Rodolfo had called his bat. This was crazy. It was unbelievable.

'Nymeria is the Lion's Mouth,' Rodolfo explained, adding to Aribella's confusion.

'Actually she's the Lioness's Mouth, even though she does have a mane!' Rosa interrupted. 'Men are always taking credit for ladies' work.'

Rodolfo nodded soberly. 'I can't argue with that.'

It seemed to Aribella that they were both rather missing the point. 'But . . . *how*? Are you saying this lion – this *lioness* – is connected to the stone Lion's Mouth on the wall of the Doge's palace?'

'Exactly.' Rodolfo smiled. 'She creates a copy of all the notes put into the Lion's Mouth. Nymeria, would you care to demonstrate?'

The lioness rose on to her four paws and stretched lethargically. She was taller than the reception desk, and Aribella again had to resist the urge to take a step backwards. She began to cough. Aribella had seen Luna cough up hairballs in the same way. But out of the lioness's throat came a balled piece of paper that fell with a puddle of spit on to the floor.

Rosa sighed. 'I do wish you wouldn't do that on the Persian rug, Nymeria.'

The bat flew off the desk, picked up the paper and dropped it into Rodolfo's hands.

'Thank you, Io.' Rodolfo unballed the paper and straightened it out on his knee, not seeming to care that he was getting gloopy lioness spit all over his trousers. '"*My brother is a stinky troll*,"' he said. 'Another wind-up. Don't think we need to worry about that one.' He balled up the paper again and tossed it into the fireplace, where it burst into flames and disappeared up the chimney.

'Want some lioness spit on your fingers?' he asked, holding out his slimy hands to Aribella. 'Great for wounds.'

Aribella blinked at him in disbelief. 'Er, no, I'm all right – thanks though.'

'Suit yourself. Your fingers should be healed by

tomorrow morning anyway.' Rodolfo slathered the goo all over his head. 'Still hoping it will help the baldness.'

Nymeria snorted as if she did not think anything could help with that, then settled back in place at the bottom of the staircase and promptly fell asleep again. Aribella watched the rhythmic rise and fall of her furry body and felt her own eyelids drooping.

'I think we'd better hurry up so we can get you to bed.' Rosa said it so kindly that Aribella felt the tiniest bit lighter. It felt wonderful to have someone care for her. Papa hadn't been able to do that properly for years.

'What about my papa?' She couldn't think about sleeping until she was sure he was safe.

'I will speak to the Elders tomorrow,' Rodolfo said gravely, 'and then I should be able to go to the Doge—'

'Tomorrow? But I can't stay here tonight when Papa's stuck in prison!' Aribella blurted. She knew she sounded ungrateful but she did not know what else to do.

'Your kind heart is admirable, child,' Rodolfo replied. 'I've no doubt your papa would be proud of you. But I assure you that if anything could be done tonight, I would have seen to it already.'

'But you must be able to do something?' Aribella persisted. 'You have a gondola that goes faster than any boat I've ever seen, a mask that can make you invisible—'

'*Unwatchable*,' Rodolfo corrected her.

'A hotel that . . . *changes*, a lioness that . . . spits,' she floundered.

Rodolfo sighed. 'The Elders have rules when it comes to Inbellis affairs.'

'Inbellis?'

'Non-Cannovacci. Humans without powers. But I promise, I will do everything I can to help your papa tomorrow.'

Aribella opened her mouth to protest again.

'You have to trust me,' he said firmly, echoing his words on the lagoon.

Rodolfo had saved Theo, hadn't he? He'd taken him home, just as he'd promised. So if he promised to help Papa, did that mean he would? She longed for someone she could trust.

'You promise?'

'I promise.' Rodolfo met her gaze, his eyes steady.

And so Aribella decided, for the second time that night, to trust him.

'Now, I'll leave you and Rosa to it if that's all right. The night is already escaping and I must read the stars,' he added, as if he was talking about reading a book. Could he really be a star-reader? It was almost too wonderful. What did the stars tell him?

Aribella removed his cloak and handed it back to him.

'Thank you. Sleep well.' He seemed suddenly exhausted as he headed upstairs, his mask in his hands, his star cloak over his arm, and Io flapping behind.

Aribella watched him go. When she turned back to the reception desk, a leather-bound book had appeared and Rosa was looking down at it.

'May I take your age, Aribella?'

'I'm thirteen . . . tomorrow actually,' she added awkwardly. Or was it today? She'd completely lost track of time.

'Oh, happy birthday!' Rosa beamed, picking up a peacock-feather quill and dipping it into a pot of blue ink, both items materializing before Aribella's eyes.

'Thanks.' Aribella stared at the inkpot and quill, then watched enviously as Rosa made a note in her book, the quill flicking back and forth. Aribella had always been fascinated by writing. Papa had taught her how to read and write a little, which was more than most children on Burano, but she still wasn't very good.

'And your power?'

'My power?'

'What can you do that makes you . . . *extraordinary*? You know, like Rodolfo can read the stars, and I can *create* things.' Rosa waved her hands and the bouquet of flowers on the desk doubled in size.

Aribella blushed, unsure what to say. 'I can . . . make fire. I mean, I think I can. It's only happened today . . .' She trailed off. It felt ridiculous saying this out loud, when earlier she thought she'd be imprisoned for admitting anything of the sort.

Rosa nodded, as if Aribella had just said she was good at swimming. She put her head on one side and a shimmering mask appeared, covering the top half of her face. The mask had tiny white moonstones arranged in intricate swirls round the edges and a large multicoloured opal in the centre. It was silver-blue – at least at first – before it caught the light and changed, turning deep purple then bright pink . . .

After everything else that had appeared in the last twenty minutes, the mask should have been the least impressive thing but something about it felt very special. As with Rodolfo's star mask, there was some-thing about Rosa's that suited her perfectly. It was clear the mask *belonged* to her.

'Can you read?' Rosa asked, handing her a large sheet of parchment.

Aribella nodded, feeling a surge of gratitude

towards Papa for teaching her.

Rosa smiled. 'You're lucky. Reading is the greatest power there is.'

'What do you mean?' Aribella asked, thinking that after Rodolfo and Rosa's powers, reading didn't sound that impressive.

'Because reading is magic! It is can transport us into other worlds or allow us to understand our own better. If I read out these rules to you, for instance, I could add whatever embellishments I liked, but you can read them for yourself and know the truth of the words. That is power. Go on, the sooner we do this the sooner we can get you to your new bedroom.'

My bedroom . . . Aribella looked down at the page.

Greetings, Novice,

Welcome to the Halfway Hotel for the Secret Society of the Cannovacci, Protectors of Venice. We kindly ask that you observe these house rules to ensure a safe and peaceful stay for all. Failure to comply may be punishable by seizure of a guest's mask and check out from the Hotel:

1. Powers must be declared at check-in.

2. Novices must not use their power without training or permission.

3. *Gondolas may only be used with their owner's permesso. Novices may not use gondolas.*

4. *No animals other than authorized companions of Elders may enter the Hotel.*

5. *Secrets of the Cannovacci must not be shared with Inbellis, excepting blood relatives and the Doge of Venice.*

We hope that you enjoy your stay at the Halfway Hotel.

The Elders of the Cannovacci

Rosa passed Aribella the peacock quill and pot of ink. Aribella had never had to write a signature before and wasn't entirely sure how it was done. She just wrote her name but wobbled her hand a bit to make it appear more grown-up. It didn't look quite right but Rosa swept the parchment away before she could change it.

'Now, I've a hot bath waiting that you should get into before you catch a chill,' she said, bustling her through a door on her left.

Aribella wasn't usually a fan of baths. However, this bathroom would have converted even the biggest bath-hater. Like the lobby, it was decadently decorated, with walls covered in mosaics of shells and coloured stones. Instead of the tin bucket Aribella had been expecting, there was a free-standing oval copper tub full of steaming water fragranced with lavender. Aribella had not smelt anything so sweet in a long time.

'I'll leave you to it,' Rosa said. 'Take your time!'

Aribella put her throbbing fingers into the warm water and the pain eased a little. She unlaced her boots, peeled off her wet socks, trousers, jumper and underwear, and slid into the water. The heat immediately soothed her aching limbs, and she lay there a while just enjoying the sensation. Then, using a scrubbing brush, she dislodged some of the dirt underneath her fingernails, and yanked a comb through her knotted hair until her eyes were stinging. Eventually she climbed out and rubbed herself dry with the thick, soft towel hanging on the stand. There was also a frilly nightgown that Theo would have laughed to see her in, but as Aribella's old clothes were damp and dirty and the nightdress was clean and dry, she put it on, along with a pair of fluffy slippers and a thick purple dressing-gown. She gathered up her damp clothes and padded back into the lobby, feeling as if she was floating on air.

Nymeria was still asleep at the base of the staircase and snoring loudly.

Rosa looked up and smiled. 'Who'd have thought

there'd be a pretty face under all that dirt? You can leave your old clothes here and I'll get them laundered.' She turned and took a gold key from one of the hooks on the row marked 'Third Floor'. It seemed to glow slightly and her fingers lingered on it briefly, as if she were uncertain. She frowned then seemed to make up her mind and held it out to Aribella. 'Third floor. The key will take you to your room. Hand it in whenever you leave the hotel so you don't lose it.'

Aribella took the heavy key. It had an orange velvet tassel and felt warm in her hand. 'Thank you.'

Rosa smiled again. 'Sweet dreams. I'll see you in the morning.'

Wary of the sleeping lioness, Aribella tiptoed towards the sweeping staircase. The enormous crystal chandelier that hung in the centre must have been made on Murano for a hefty price. Above it, a slice of dark sky was visible through a hexagonal window in the ceiling.

Oil lamps lined the staircase, lighting her way as she climbed. Aribella was too exhausted to take much in, except for soft carpet, portraits and seemingly endless stairs. This was a world away from Papa's tiny cottage. She hoped he would be safe tonight. She hoped everyone on the islands would be safe too, and that there were no more of those ghastly spectres. She thought of that horrible mark on Theo's skin. Thank goodness Rodolfo had saved him. What if he hadn't been there with that vinegar stuff? She didn't want to think about it.

She reached the third floor and stopped in surprise. A boy stood on the landing. *Half-stood,* she realized with shock. For while half of the boy was in the hall-way, the other half seemed to be on the other side of a closed door.

Aribella gasped and the boy's eyes snapped open.

'What? What is it?' he cried. The other half of his body appeared through the door as he whirled round. Now all of him was visible, Aribella could see that he was lanky, with blond hair that stuck up at odd angles like straw. The sleeves of his nightshirt were too short. He looked about her age.

'Hello,' she said nervously. 'Er . . . are you all right?'

The boy groaned and slapped one hand to his fore-head. 'Oh no, I was sleepwalking again, wasn't I? I keep trying to stop but I tell you, being able to walk through walls makes it ten times worse . . .' His eyes narrowed. 'You're new, I presume?'

'I, er . . . just arrived.'

'Well, you gave me quite a fright.'

'You gave me a fright too!'

The boy grinned. 'Welcome anyway. I'm Fin.'

'Aribella.'

'Nice to meet you, Aribella. Looking forward to meeting you properly in the morning. We'd better head to bed before Rosa catches us, or worse, Jacapo. See you tomorrow.' Fin dissolved through the door, leaving Aribella alone on the landing with her mouth hanging open.

For a moment, she stood there staring. Then she went to the door and ran her fingers over the wood. It was solid. She felt as if her entire world had been flipped upside down. Nothing made sense. But a small voice in her said: *You always thought there was magic in the world and now you're seeing that it's true.*

The key buzzed in her hand, as if to remind her that it was bedtime. It swung like a compass needle and she followed its direction down the hall until it buzzed in her hand outside a door. She put the key in the lock. It was a perfect fit and turned easily with a click. The door swung open.

Aribella blinked at the beautiful bedroom beyond. A single candle flickered on a nightstand, illuminating light blue wallpaper intricately patterned with ornate silver flowers, trees and birds. There was more furniture in the bedroom than in Papa's entire cottage: two nightstands either side of a grand four-poster bed, a large oak wardrobe, a mirrored dressing table and two elegant armchairs that flanked a fireplace. The bedroom was enormous. Was all this space really just for her? Giddy excitement filled Aribella's chest. To think that she – the daughter of a lacemaker – would be sleeping here, in the grandest palazzo on the Grand Canal! But where was Papa sleeping? This thought dampened her happiness but she tried to tell herself that all would be fine once Rodolfo had been to the Doge. He had promised.

Aribella shook off the slippers and dressing-gown, and hauled herself up on to the mattress. Tugging back the heavy quilt, she slipped gratefully between the soft silk sheets. She barely kept her eyes open long enough to blow out the candle, and soon she fell into a deep sleep.

9

When Aribella woke she was confused. Instead of looking up at spiders' webs in her dusty bedroom in Burano, she found herself staring up at a beautiful silk canopy. Her heart leapt. So, it hadn't been a dream! In her exhaustion, she hadn't thought to draw the curtains last night, and the morning sunlight bathed everything in a warm glow.

Aribella stared around the room in dizzy happiness. The blue-and-silver wallpaper was even more beautiful in the daylight, and there was a large cuckoo clock above the door she hadn't noticed the night before. The vase of freshly cut wildflowers that had appeared on the night-stand in place of the candle must have been Rosa's work, she thought.

Aribella stretched and found the stinging in her

fingers had reduced to a dull ache. She felt the edge of something hard under her pillow and pulled out a chocolate wrapped in gold paper. The chocolate was squashed but Aribella unwrapped it excitedly and popped it in her mouth, groaning aloud at the rich, gooey sweetness. She couldn't remember the last time she'd eaten chocolate. Untangling herself from the quilt and sheets, Aribella pressed her feet into the slippers again and padded towards the grand window to peek out.

It was a glorious autumn morning. The sky was brilliantly blue and the Grand Canal sparkled. On one side, the indigo flags that marked the San Marco district waved, and on the other, the yellow San Polo flags puffed back. Market barges slid along the water below, but none of their passengers looked up or even gave the hotel so much as a second glance. They probably still saw the Halfway the way she'd seen it last night: broken and dilapidated. If only they knew!

She gazed across the rooftops of the floating city. The Republic's domes, spires and towers glittered in the morning sun, like jewels in a crown. Between them were countless canals, bridges and boats, and windows gleamed like the lagoon itself, so that the sea seemed to be inside every house. Aribella strained her eyes towards the distant horizon. Burano lay there somewhere, too far to see.

The sound of her door slamming open made Aribella jump and spin round.

A short, fierce-looking girl with curly hair ran into the room, and crouched beside her bed, looking underneath it. Aribella was about to ask her who she was and what she was doing when the girl made a loud mewing sound. She sounded *exactly* like a cat . . . Aribella took a step backwards and knocked into the window.

At the sound, the girl sprang up at once and glared. She had beautiful green eyes that were orange-flecked, with gold edges. 'What are you doing in here?'

Again, Aribella was taken aback. 'Rosa said it was my room.'

The girl wrinkled her nose. 'Well, don't look under the bed!'

'I wasn't planning to . . .' Aribella muttered, confused by the girl's hostility. Wasn't this meant to be her room? Again, the feeling of being out of place niggled at her.

All of a sudden, a black ball of fur shot out from under the bed and launched itself at Aribella's ankles. It was a cat! And not just any cat . . .

'Luna!' Aribella exclaimed joyfully. 'How in the lagoon did you get in here?' She picked Luna up and hugged her, so delighted to see her that for a moment she forgot the other girl was there.

'She's your cat?' The girl sounded surprised.

'Oh no, not really! She's a stray from Burano. Me and my friend named her Luna as we only used to see her at night.' Aribella stopped because thinking about Theo made her heart ache.

The other girl raised an eyebrow. 'How did you get her in?'

'I didn't,' Aribella replied quickly, remembering Rosa's no animals rule. 'I've no idea how she found me.'

'You didn't smuggle her in?'

'No!'

The girl sank down on to Aribella's bed with a sigh. 'I wish you had. Then I'd know how to do it. No animal has ever got into Halfway without Rosa's permission. She's so funny about Novices having pets but I keep telling her I should be an exception. My power is being able to talk to animals, after all, and how can I do that if there's only snoring Nymeria and Io. My room's next door and I heard a meow so I knew there was a cat in here. You must have been asleep.'

Talk to animals . . . Could this really be the girl's power? If so, it was the best so far. She had always wondered what Luna was thinking.

'That's a wonderful power!' she said.

The girl smiled coyly. 'Some people don't think so. They say animals don't have anything to say that's worth hearing.'

'That's nonsense. Animals are so intelligent.'

'That's what I think,' the girl agreed passionately. 'If you ask me there are plenty of humans who don't say a thing worth hearing, yet *they* are the ones who talk the most.'

In spite of warming a little, she was still eyeing Aribella with distrust, until Aribella stroked Luna in her favourite place under her chin. When Luna purred loudly the girl seemed to relax.

'I've known Luna most of my life and have always wanted to talk to her,' Aribella said. 'Could you do me a favour? Could you ask if she's seen Theo?'

'Who's Theo?'

'My friend. He was . . . sick,' she said, deciding it was easier to say this than to try to explain what had happened last night. 'Could you?'

'Oh, all right.' The girl meowed a few times and Luna meowed back. The girl looked puzzled and shook her head. 'I'm sorry but she's not making a lot of sense. Or it's some kind of weird cat dialect that I don't know. I can't even get her to tell me her real name.'

'Well, I'll just carry on calling her Luna then.'

Luna meowed.

The girl laughed. 'Well, she seems to like that name and it's obvious she likes you. And anyone who is a friend of animals is a friend of mine.' She held out her hand. 'I'm Seffie. Persephone really, but don't call me that if you want to keep all your teeth.'

Aribella almost laughed, but Seffie looked so fierce that she nodded seriously instead. Seffie, however, must have found something in Aribella's startled expression amusing, because she cocked her head to one side and suddenly laughed herself. The effect was amazing. It was as if curtains had been lifted. Her dark scowl dissolved and her face became full of sunshine. She had a laugh that came right from her belly.

'What's your name?'

'Aribella.'

Luna purred louder and Seffie meowed. Again the sound was uncannily cat-like, but this time Luna didn't respond.

Seffie sighed. 'I really wish she'd tell me how she managed to get past Rosa.'

'Can you talk to all animals?' Aribella asked.

Seffie smiled mischievously. All traces of her earlier hostility were gone and she seemed to have decided that they were going to be friends. 'Most. I can talk dog, monkey, horse . . . I speak some languages better than others. Always had a problem with giraffe, and sea creatures can be tricky – all those bubbles!' She shook her head and her curls bounced everywhere.

Aribella's mind was boggled by the fact that Seffie could talk to *one* animal let alone all the different kinds Seffie had just listed. She didn't even know what a giraffe was!

'What's your power then?' Seffie asked.

Aribella told her about the sparks.

'Oh, fire is such a cool power!'

It was Aribella's turn to smile. She was still getting used to the idea of having a power, and far from feeling good about it, it scared her. She envied Seffie's ability to talk to animals. It seemed a lot less destructive then setting things alight. Would she ever feel as positively about her power as Seffie did?

'It started yesterday,' she explained.

'Yesterday?' Seffie's eyes widened. 'But that means . . . wait, is it your thirteenth birthday today?'

Aribella nodded. 'Although—'

'Why didn't you say anything? Happy Birthday!'

'Thanks.' Aribella smiled and resisted the urge to point out that she hadn't really had the chance. Luna started to wriggle so she put her down. 'But how did you know?'

'The day before thirteenth birthdays is when most

powers first appear. I was invited here soon after my birthday too. Fifteenth of July, don't forget it. My parents are part of a travelling circus. They were so surprised when I started chatting to the animals! I really miss them,' she added.

'Your parents?'

'No!' Seffie wrinkled her nose. 'Well, maybe a bit. Truth is, I think Mama and Papa were relieved when Rodolfo explained I was a Cannovacci. They thought I'd gone crazy, growling and hissing all the time! No, it's the animals I miss most.' She sighed and sat cross-legged on Aribella's bed. 'So, tell me, how did it happen for you?'

Aribella told her the story of Gian in the market. She was surprised at how quickly she'd grown comfortable in Seffie's company and spoke freely, though she stopped short of telling her what had happened on the lagoon afterwards.

'Don't worry,' Seffie said once she'd finished. 'Everyone's powers are out of control at first. For weeks, I was speaking duck when I was trying to speak sparrow. Can you imagine? Then I got my mask and things were heaps better.'

Proudly, Seffie took out a mask from the yellow shoulder bag she was carrying. It had pointed ears and its colourful face was covered with feathers and fur.

Butterfly wings were painted on either cheek.

'It's beautiful!' Aribella said.

'Thanks. Every Cannovacci gets one – and only one. They help you control your powers. As well as making you unwatchable when you need to be, and all sorts of other things.'

It could help control her power? That was a relief! And if it could make her unwatchable, maybe that meant she could go back and visit Theo.

'You'll get one soon. Any day now. The Mask Maker doesn't usually wait long.'

'I hope mine's half as nice as yours.'

Seffie grinned. 'It will be. The Mask Maker's a proud man. He's always trying to outdo himself. So what did your family say about you being Cannovacci?'

Aribella's throat grew tight.

'Are you all right?' Seffie asked.

'Yes, sorry, I'm fine . . .' Then, because she wanted to be honest with her new friend, Aribella added, 'My mama died when I was three and my papa, he's—' Again, her throat tightened. Luna mewed softly and rubbed her head against Aribella's legs. Her familiar, warm softness was reassuring. 'He's in the palace prison.'

'What? Why?'

Seffie eyes widened as Aribella told her about last

night. Talking about the guards, the lagoon and the spectre in the sunlight-filled room felt silly, as if Aribella was explaining a nightmare, though it had been horribly real at the time.

'And Rodolfo knew what it was at once?'

Aribella nodded.

'I've never heard of anything like that before. Sounds really scary!'

'It was,' Aribella agreed. 'I hope there are no more of them out there.'

'I'm sure if there are, Rodolfo and the other Elders will find them. The stars tell him the future so if there's any danger coming he'll know about it and find a way to stop it. With him and Nymeria we should all be safe.'

So it was the future that Rodolfo was reading. Aribella hoped Seffie was right.

There was a loud *dong* as the clock above the door struck the hour and a yellow cuckoo shot out. Aribella jumped and Seffie burst out laughing again. Luna pawed at the balcony doors, so Aribella let her out. They watched her jump from balcony to balcony, working her way down to the jetty.

'That must be how she got in,' Aribella said.

Seffie frowned. 'Weird if she did. There's more protection on this place than you can see.'

Aribella thought of the hotel's changing appearance and didn't doubt it.

'We'd better go down to breakfast. Come on, get dressed. My tummy is rumbling so loudly it sounds like Nymeria's snoring in there.'

'Right, yes.' Aribella looked for her old clothes but remembered she'd left them with Rosa last night. Her stomach twisted at the thought of meeting the rest of the Halfway's guests in her frilly nightdress.

Seffie was wearing a beautiful pair of yellow pantaloons that suited her perfectly. 'Check the wardrobe,' she said, smiling mischievously.

Aribella looked at the large oak wardrobe. Carefully, she opened the heavy door and gasped at the rainbow of silk and satin dresses hanging inside. 'But they can't all be for me?'

'Who else would they be for?'

Aribella had never seen so many beautiful clothes. They were a world away from the coarse trousers, holey jumpers and ripped second-hand shirts she was used to. She picked out a dark blue dress with long draped sleeves and a ribboned bodice. It was the simplest item in the wardrobe but still looked like something a princess would wear.

It took a while to lace the bodice but Seffie helped. When it was done, Aribella looked in the mirror and barely recognized herself.

Feeling a bit foolish, she almost took the dress off, but before she could Seffie exclaimed, '*Che bella!*' and pulled her out of the door.

10

They descended the staircase and Aribella soon forgot all about the dress. There were so many beautiful and curious things to look at. Even the stairwell was full of countless treasures that she'd been too tired to appreciate the night before. She kept getting left behind by an increasingly exasperated Seffie, as she stopped to examine the gold-framed portraits that lined the walls. Some looked centuries old, but they all had something in common: every single person wore a mask just as exquisite as Rodolfo's, Rosa's or Seffie's – even in paint – decorated in unique arrangements of feathers, sequins and jewels.

'Graduation portraits,' Seffie explained, doubling back to where Aribella had stopped by a painting of a handsome man with a black half-mask that sliced diagonally across his face. He had straight dark hair, pale skin and high cheekbones. White petals lay on the floor below the portrait in a delicate pattern. Underneath the painting was written a single word: *Zio*.

'Graduation from what?'

'Halfway. We'll get our own portraits when we're eighteen.'

'Really?' Aribella's skin tingled.

'Yes, when we've done all our Novice training and become Elders.'

Aribella looked down at the ground. 'Why does this one have petals under it?'

'Oh.' Seffie looked over her shoulder and lowered her voice. 'Well, it's a bit of a story. I don't know exactly what happened but apparently he was *murdered* – by another Cannovacci.'

'*What?*'

'Yes, it's all very hush-hush.'

'Who murdered him?'

Seffie shrugged. 'I don't know, it was years ago. Come on, Ari, I'm starving,' she groaned, tugging on Aribella's arm.

Ari was what Theo called her. It was strange to hear Seffie use it with such familiarity after less than an hour together, but Aribella found she liked it. She pulled her eyes away from the paintings and let Seffie drag her down the stairs.

On the first floor, a mouth-watering aroma of freshly baked bread and sweet pastries filled the air. Seffie marched up to a pair of intricately carved oak doors. A sign read: *POLITE NOTICE: No masks to be worn in the dining room.* Aribella could hear a buzz of conversation. Her stomach fluttered with nerves as Seffie shoved the doors open without hesitation.

Aribella had never been in a hotel dining room before, but she was still certain that this one must be the best in the entire world. On one side of the room, sunlight streamed through three floor-to-ceiling windows. The large balcony beyond was full of colourful flowers, and the view over the Grand Canal was similar to the one that Aribella had from her new bedroom window. Circular tables were covered with lace tablecloths, sparkling crystal glasses, and neatly laid-out cutlery. Jugs of bright orange juice and bowls of sugar sat on every single one. Aribella stared in astonishment.

About fifty guests of all ages were seated round the tables, chatting and tucking into pastries. A beautiful lady with pale skin, blue eyes and a long plait of white-blonde hair caught Aribella's eye. She sat next to a dark-haired lady with braids piled on top of her head and colourful scarves wrapped round her shoulders.

They were chatting like old friends.

Aribella looked for Rodolfo, anxious to ask him if he had any news on Papa, but he was nowhere to be seen.

'The grown-ups are Elders,' Seffie informed her. 'I'm sure you'll meet them all eventually. Most are nice, just don't get on the wrong side of Jacapo.' She nodded to a small, harassed-looking man with a red face and a few strands of wispy white hair that had been brushed over his head sideways in a bad attempt to hide his baldness. Aribella remembered the similar warning Fin had given her about Jacapo last night.

'Is he in charge?'

Seffie wrinkled her nose. 'No. It's meant to be a democracy, but Jacapo is the one who enforces rules the most. He's a real pain. Best to avoid him.'

'What's his power?' Aribella asked. 'Being bossy?'

Seffie cackled. 'You'd think! He can control sound. Although he's so boring, everyone just stops talking at the sight of him anyway.'

She steered Aribella to the centre of the room, where a large buffet table was so laden with trays of golden pastries that it looked about to topple. Glazed spirals topped with toasted sugar were piled next to delicate almond-flaked twists and fat buns studded with raisins the size of buttons. Aribella's mouth watered. To her delight, she spotted some folded squares of pastry drizzled with chocolate that she'd seen at the market and always longed to taste.

Seffie followed Aribella's gaze and piled several of the chocolate-drizzled squares on to a plate. 'Go on, have one now!'

Aribella didn't need to be told twice. It was more delicious than she ever could have imagined – a perfect mix of crispy and gooey – and instantly became her favourite food in the entire world.

'Here, try this too,' said Seffie, handing her another pastry that was shell-shaped.

Aribella took a bite. It tasted of candied lemon and was just as delicious.

'Good, aren't they?' Seffie smiled. 'Take as many as you want.'

When their plates were piled high with as many pastries as they could carry, Seffie led Aribella to a table by the windows where two boys and two girls were sitting.

'*Ciao*, Aribella. How did you sleep?' one of the boys asked, putting his book down.

'Morning, Fin!' Aribella said, pleased to know some-one already.

Seffie frowned. 'How do you two know each other?'

'We met last night,' Fin said. 'I managed to sleep-walk right through my bedroom door and into the corridor. When I woke up, she was staring right at me!'

One of the girls laughed. Her long, dark hair fell to her waist and she was wearing a beautiful emerald-green dress. 'What a great introduction!' she exclaimed.

'Don't encourage him, Julietta,' the younger girl next to her said. She had short spiky hair and an expression to match. She was wearing plain trousers and a shirt buttoned right up to her chin that was secured with an old-fashioned gold brooch. 'Using your power without permission is against the—'

'Rules,' the others all chimed together, laughing.

The spiky girl's face went beetroot.

'I know, Helena,' Fin went on. 'It wasn't like I did it deliberately. The Elders should understand. Every-one's powers are a bit out of control to start with. Except yours, of course. Whatever it really is.'

Helena scowled. 'My power is my own business. Anyway, you should tell Rosa what happened.'

'If you tell her I'll get Bruno to beat you up.'

'I'm not beating anyone up!' the other boy protested. Though he was large and stocky, his voice was soft and he looked hurt.

'Suit yourself.' Fin shrugged and picked up his book again.

'Enough, you two,' said Julietta. 'Aribella's going to

think we're weird.'

'We are weird,' Fin said from behind his book.

Julietta rolled her eyes and smiled up at Aribella. 'Welcome to the mad house. Do sit down.'

'Er, thanks.' Aribella smiled back shyly.

Bruno groaned as he picked up his spoon and it bent in his grip. 'Not again!'

Aribella could make a pretty good guess at Bruno's power . . . She wondered what Julietta and Helena could do. Why didn't Helena want to talk about her power?

'So how were you found?' Julietta asked.

Aribella licked sugar from her lips. 'My name came through the Lion's Mouth.'

Helena's eyes widened and even Fin looked up from his book.

'You're the first to be found like that for years,' said Fin. 'Most of the names that come through the Lion's Mouth are just pranks. One generation of Cannovacci almost got rid of it altogether.'

Aribella thought back to last night: the image of the huge lioness spitting out the paper came back to her like a strange dream. She reached for the orange juice, her mind elsewhere, and the jug slipped in her hand as she poured. Orange juice went everywhere. The others pushed their chairs back and Fin lifted his book above his head just in time.

Aribella's face grew hot. 'Oh, I'm so sorry . . .' Before she could even try to stop it, a spark shot from her index finger and caught the edge of the tablecloth. She jumped backwards as more flames appeared.

Moving so fast that she became a blur, Julietta grabbed a jug of water from another table and threw it over the flames, which went out with a wet sizzle. Julietta stopped being a blur and Aribella saw that she was now wearing a curved bronze half-mask with cheetah spots across the cheeks and two bronze wings sticking up on either side. Julietta must have pulled the mask out of the now-open shoulder bag hanging off her chair and put it on so quickly that Aribella hadn't even seen her do it.

Aribella gasped. 'Thank you!'

Julietta shrugged. 'My power is speed. Can be useful.'

Seffie leant over, picked up a sodden pastry from her plate and grinned. 'Thanks, Julietta! Aribella almost set fire to my last *sfogliatella* but you drowned it instead!'

The others laughed, except Helena, but stopped immediately when Jacapo approached their table.

'What's going on over here?' he asked, surveying them with his small eyes.

'Just a little accident. All under control now,' Seffie said brightly. 'It's Aribella's first day. We were welcoming her.'

Jacapo turned his gaze to Aribella. He did not offer any welcoming words.

'It's not a proper Cannovacci first day without a little excitement, is it?' a sing-song voice said from behind them.

Aribella turned to see Rosa. She was wearing another beautiful dress. This one was purple with pearls round the neckline. The key keeper clapped her hands and an enormous chocolate cake covered in candles appeared out of thin air. '*Happy Birthday to you . . .*' she sang.

The entire dining room joined in, and Aribella did the same, quietly wondering who shared her birthday.

'*Happy Birthday, dear ARIBELLA!*' everyone sang.

Aribella blinked. The cake was for her?

Rosa gestured for her to blow out the thirteen candles on top, which she did to tumultuous applause. Seffie clapped Aribella on the back so hard that she almost had a coughing fit, and Rosa cut the cake and handed it round.

'How are you feeling this morning, Aribella?' she asked.

'Well, thank you.'

'Good. Well, after you've had your cake would you please come with me? There's a meeting of the Elders and Rodolfo wants you to join them.'

The other Novices stopped mid-mouthful and exchanged looks. The warm feeling of belonging Aribella had experienced suddenly faded. She was still different – a Novice of the Lion's Mouth. She noticed the Elders were beginning to leave the dining room. Rodolfo would want her to tell them about last night.

Aribella nodded stiffly. The pastries were sitting in her stomach uncomfortably now. She didn't want to talk about the spectre again, but she knew she had to – and it would be a chance to find out if there was any news of Papa. So she quickly finished her cake, wiped her mouth and said goodbye to the others.

Seffie gave her arm a small squeeze. 'It'll be fine.'

Aribella nodded, half wishing she would come with her. But the feeling of Seffie's squeeze lingered on her skin. It felt good to have a friend.

11

Aribella followed Rosa down to the lobby, where Nymeria was still sleeping, and through a door opposite the bathroom. This led into a luxurious lounge. The dark wood panelling on the walls reminded Aribella of a ship's cabin. Purple and orange armchairs were arranged carefully about the room, with mahogany coffee tables between them.

All the Elders from the dining room seemed to be there, including the lady with the white-blonde plait and the lady with the braids. So too was the scowling Jacapo. Aribella's stomach clenched.

'Welcome, Aribella,' said Rodolfo. He was the only Elder standing, dressed this morning in a sky-blue waistcoat that, like his cloak, was covered in stars. Io was hanging from the mantelpiece, apparently sleeping, his little leathery wings wrapped round him. 'You slept well?'

Aribella nodded. She could not say the same for Rodolfo, who looked exhausted. Had he been up all night reading the stars? Aribella was starting to wonder how she *had* slept so well, given all her worries about Papa, Theo and the spectre . . . Perhaps the sweet-smelling bubbles in the bathtub had had something to do with it. She glanced back at Rosa.

'These are the Halfway Hotel's Elders,' Rodolfo continued. 'There are many of us, so I won't waste time on introductions now if that's all right with every-one. Aribella looks far too nervous to remember names anyway.'

There was a murmur of laughter, but only a small one. The atmosphere in the room was tense.

Rodolfo became serious too. 'Now, Aribella, could you please describe, in your own words, what you saw on the lagoon last night?'

Every face in the room turned to her. Jacapo watched her coldly, his eyes flicking back and forth between her and Rodolfo. Beside him the woman with the silver-blonde plait was looking concerned.

Aribella found her throat had gone dry and swallowed several times. 'Well, first the moon . . . changed colour. It went red.'

Rodolfo nodded gravely. 'Yes, the blood moon. We know about that. It happens rarely, but when it does it signals that the boundary between the world of the living and the world of the dead is vulnerable.'

So Gian hadn't been talking as much rubbish as she and Theo had thought. Could there really be such a thin line between the two worlds? The idea filled Aribella with fear. She thought again of the spectre and shivered.

'And then what happened?' Rodolfo prompted.

'I . . . I was rowing on the lagoon, with my friend, and there was this strange mist and this . . . *thing* . . . this skull came out of the mist and bit my friend. Signore Rodolfo gave him this vinegar that healed him.'

The room had gone completely silent. Aribella's sore fingers tingled and she balled her hands into fists behind her back. Now was not the time to burst into flames again.

It was Rodolfo who broke the silence first. 'You remember, Marquesa,' he said, turning to the lady with the braids and colourful scarves, 'that after I read the stars last month, I asked you to brew me a batch of Four Thieves Vinegar, just in case?'

Marquesa nodded. 'Of course I do,' she said in a low, husky voice. 'It's an extremely difficult potion to brew. Takes twelve hours and the ingredients are hard to come by.'

'Which is why you only made me a small amount,' Rodolfo replied. 'But I would suggest you make more, as much and as soon as you can.' His expression was so serious that Aribella was frightened all over again. Did Rodolfo think there would be another attack?

'Surely that's not necessary!' exclaimed Jacapo. 'One spectre attack, while unfortunate, doesn't mean there will be more.' He glanced at Aribella. 'It may not even be true!'

'But this is impossible!' The speaker was the lady with the blonde plait. 'Spectres can't move from the world of the dead.'

'I know it seems so, Ursula,' Rodolfo replied, 'and I don't understand it either, but I'm afraid it has happened. We have to be careful. Remember the Black Death . . .'

'The Black Death was a plague! Nothing more to it,' Jacapo snapped.

'That's what we've told ourselves for centuries, but many believe that it was the last time the spectres crossed the boundary. That it wasn't really a plague, but spectres feasting on souls.'

A murmur swept through the room.

'Forgive me, Rodolfo,' Jacapo said, rising to his feet and drawing himself up to his full height, still barely level with Rodolfo's chest. 'But these are just stories. The boundary is strong and we Cannovacci have been protecting it and Venice for centuries.'

There were sounds of agreement.

'If it is strong, then why is the water rising far more than usual?' Rodolfo boomed.

The room went quiet again.

'The *acqua alta*,' someone muttered. 'It happens every year.'

'It's too early for that,' Rodolfo countered. 'And the water is much higher.'

Aribella felt sure her presence had been forgotten. She was struggling to keep up with the conversation.

'I have seen spectres in the stars, as I've already told you,' Rodolfo went on. 'There is a darkness coming, a darkness that, if it is not stopped, spells doom for all of us – for Venice, and quite possibly the world.'

Another stunned hush followed. Elders shifted nervously in their seats.

'What sort of doom?' asked Ursula, her voice trembling.

Rodolfo shook his head gravely. 'I do not know.'

'But you're the star-reader,' Jacapo said mockingly. 'Aren't you meant to know?'

On the mantelpiece, Io flexed his wings.

Rodolfo frowned. 'The stars are strange. There are

102

messages in them I have never seen before, which I do not yet fully understand. But I have a theory.'

'Which is?' Jacapo's tone remained sceptical.

Rodolfo paused. 'Zio.'

The word hit the room like a bolt of lightning. Elders were on their feet in uproar, knocking over glasses of water and cups of coffee. Ursula burst into tears and Marquesa put an arm round her. Aribella's brain whirled. Zio was the name of the man in the portrait with the petals below it, the one who had been murdered.

Jacapo raised his hands. '*Silenzio!*'

The room instantly fell quiet and Aribella wondered if Jacapo had used his power to control sound.

Jacapo shot the star-reader a scathing look. 'Rodolfo, really? Are you really going to drag all this up again? We had enough of your ridiculous theories ten years ago! Zio was murdered, Rodolfo, *murdered*. I know you find it hard to believe that Clara did it, but it's the truth. And you making up preposterous conspiracies does not help anyone.'

There was a loud thump. Ursula had fainted and fallen off her chair.

Marquesa quickly knelt beside her and rummaged in her cloak. She took out a handkerchief and a small jar of powder. She sprinkled the powder into the handkerchief and placed it to Ursula's nose. Ursula revived instantly. She pushed the handkerchief away, spluttering.

'Are you all right, Ursula?' Rodolfo asked, but Jacapo turned on him at once.

'Look what you've done!' he snapped. 'It is not wise to speak ill of Zio, Rodolfo. He was a victim. It's time you were honest with yourself and faced up to what Clara really was.'

Aribella's head was spinning. She wished someone would just explain, but it seemed, from the shifty looks around the room, that the Elders were skirting round the edges of a secret they would far rather forget.

'Why were you alone on the lagoon last night, anyway?' Jacapo snapped.

'I was following a name from the Lion's Mouth.'

'Without discussing it with the rest of the Elders?'

Rodolfo's eyes narrowed. 'What exactly are you accusing me of, Jacapo?'

'You didn't follow protocol. You're meant to report Lion's Mouth names to the Council of Elders so that we can elect a person to collect the Novice. Why did you take it upon yourself? Did you see something in the stars you're not telling us?' Jacapo's eyes flashed.

Ursula let out another whimper.

'Of course not,' Rodolfo replied, but Aribella

thought she saw the tiniest flicker of something change in his expression, like a cloud skidding across the moon. He was definitely hiding something. But what? She'd decided to trust Rodolfo and needed to believe he was going to help Papa . . . But *was* it suspicious that he'd been on the lagoon alone last night?

'Look, I apologize for that, I do, but there was little time. The Doge's guards had already captured Aribella's father, which brings us to another matter,' Rodolfo said, moving on smoothly. 'He is currently in the palace prisons awaiting trial. I ask to be allowed to intervene in order to stop an innocent man rotting in prison, or worse.'

Aribella's chest tightened. *Poor Papa.*

'You know we don't involve ourselves in Inbellis affairs,' Jacapo snapped.

'*Unless absolutely necessary,*' Rodolfo countered. 'And in this case it is necessary, given that the man in question is Aribella's father and Aribella is a Cannovacci—'

'*He* is still Inbellis.'

It was as if the walls of the lounge were closing in. Aribella had been so eager to know when the Cannovacci would save Papa – now it turned out the question was whether they *would*.

'Please, help him,' she blurted. 'I'll do anything.'

Jacapo's expression remained stony. 'Send the

Novice away.'

Aribella felt a gentle hand on her shoulder. 'Come on,' Rosa said softly. 'The Elders need to discuss this . . . Perhaps it is best you leave while we do.'

'But I should be here,' Aribella gasped, shrugging Rosa off. Tears were already welling in her eyes and she blinked them back. She did not want to cry in front of the Elders.

'I promised to help your papa,' Rodolfo said, his blue eyes steady. 'I will keep my word.'

Aribella shot Jacapo and the other Elders one last pleading look as Rosa ushered her out into the cool lobby.

The door of the lounge closed behind her with a heavy thud.

12

ribella nearly jumped out of her skin when Seffie popped up behind the reception desk.

'What did they say, Ari?' she whispered. 'It was hard to hear through the door.'

'That's the point! You're not supposed to hear if you're not invited to the meeting!' Helena's voice hissed angrily from the landing above. 'You shouldn't be eavesdropping.'

'Well, you're eavesdropping on me, Helena,' Seffie pointed out.

'I'm trying to stop you from breaking rules! Oh, fine, get checked-out of Halfway, see if I care.' Helena's footsteps stomped away up the staircase.

Seffie rolled her eyes. 'She's such a goody-two-shoes. They won't check me out,' she added, with a toothy grin. 'I'm far too dangerous to be unleashed on the streets. But tell me what happened. Was it about the spectre?'

Aribella nodded, but didn't trust herself to speak.

'It's all right if you don't want to talk about it,' Seffie said understandingly. She stiffened guiltily as the lounge door opened again and Rosa's head appeared round it.

'I thought I heard voices! What are you doing lurking out here, Persephone?'

'I, er – just came to give Aribella the grand tour,' Seffie blurted. 'Didn't I, Ari?'

Aribella nodded uncertainly.

'Well, I think you've done the lobby thoroughly.' Rosa arched her eyebrows but she gave them a tired smile. 'Why don't you show Aribella the rest of the hotel?'

'Great idea.' Seffie nodded. 'Might as well actually give you a tour now,' she said once Rosa had shut the door, and she linked her arm through Aribella's.

Aribella loved the instant closeness of this gesture, the way it tied her and Seffie together as they climbed the stairs. Aribella would never dream of linking arms with anyone else, even Theo – and especially someone she'd only met the previous evening. But Seffie was so comfortable in her own skin that it did not cross her mind for a second that Aribella might reject such a gesture, and Aribella was sure that, even if she had, Seffie would not take it personally as Aribella might have done. Seffie was confident enough for both of them and this made everything simple. Seffie had decided they were going to be friends, so they were.

Seffie didn't press Aribella on the Elders' meeting, and instead distracted her with the tour, which took most of the morning. The hotel turned out to have more nooks, crannies and hidden delights than she'd thought. Indeed, the interior of Halfway was far bigger than the exterior suggested, and Aribella's head hurt trying to make sense of it. She'd only counted three tiers of windows from the outside last night, but inside there seemed to be four floors, and on each of these floors the corridors extended much further than seemed possible.

'Don't try to work it out,' Seffie warned, when Aribella mentioned this. 'Halfway is like a maze. It doesn't make any sense, but that's why it's great.'

The ground floor was where the formal meeting rooms were. The first floor was for informal communal areas – the dining room, two more lounges, and a beautiful reading room, to name just a few. The second floor was for training rooms, and the third floor was where the Novices' bedrooms were. Seffie showed

Aribella her own bedroom. It was like a jungle, with green leaf-patterned wallpaper and real plants and vines everywhere.

'Novices get rooms, Elders get suites,' Seffie explained. 'If they want them.' Rosa says that as long as a Cannovacci is alive and part of the Cannovacci, a room exists for them at the Halfway. When they die or are checked-out, the room passes back to the hotel, ready to be made up for its new guest. That's called a turnover.'

Seffie was most excited to show Aribella the rooftop, which was accessed by a rickety ladder.

'This is where I come to chat to the birds. Rodolfo reads the stars here too,' Seffie announced once they had emerged into cold wind and bright sunshine. 'You can see Venus and Mars on a clear night.'

The roof was covered in rugs and cushions, and a number of telescopes were set up at different angles. The view over the city was incredible, but Aribella could not stop staring at a complicated-looking star chart chalked on the stone floor. She wondered if any of those markings had predicted the spectre, and shivered.

Seffie seemed to sense this change in her mood. 'Let's go down to the basement next. I can show you the swimming pool.'

The distraction worked. 'What?' A basement swimming pool in Venice? It was unheard of!

'It's for us to practise breathing underwater with our masks. It will be more fun once you get your mask, of course, then we can talk underwater too.'

'Talk underwater?' Aribella spluttered. 'Your mask . . . lets you do that too?'

'Of course,' Seffie said as if this was no big deal.

'What *don't* the masks do?'

'Help you smuggle animals into Halfway. Come on.' Seffie linked arms again and steered Aribella back to the ladder. Aribella wondered if she'd ever stop being amazed. There was something new to discover every minute.

When they reached the lobby, Seffie hopped over the sleeping Nymeria and the reception desk, and took the swimming pool key from the gold hooks. There were only two on the row marked 'Basement'.

'Rosa doesn't mind if I take the swimming pool key,' she said airily. 'It's only the Novices that really use it. But that's the only one – if you try to take someone else's room key, you'll set off Nymeria.'

As if to agree, the lioness let out an extra-loud snore.

Seffie led them through a heavy, bolted door that led down to the basement. Roughly cut stone steps descended into a corridor that was lit with torches.

'The Elders never come down here,' Seffie said, as they went deeper and deeper below ground. And after a while: 'Oh, I think I've taken a wrong turn.'

They had stopped at a door which seemed to be the end of a corridor. Seffie peered closely at it and tried the swimming pool key. It didn't buzz in her hand, as Aribella's room key had done, and wouldn't turn either. Seffie shrugged. 'Wrong door. The swimming pool must be the other way, come on. It's worth it, I promise.'

She was right. Bathing suits and towels were laid out ready for them to use and it was great fun splashing around in the mosaicked pool. Seffie was a great swimmer. Aribella didn't have a mask so she couldn't breathe underwater for long but she watched in awe as Seffie put on her mask and didn't resurface for almost ten minutes. The sooner she could get her own mask the better.

After an hour, Aribella and Seffie, with fingers like pickled cucumbers, emerged back into the lobby. Their hair dripped with water and they were wearing matching grins.

Rosa called out, 'Oh, there you are, Aribella. The meeting's finally over – Rodolfo will be out in a minute to talk to you. In the meantime, here's something for you.'

She handed Aribella a thick white envelope. On the

front, Aribella's name was written in swirling gold ink. Aribella had never had a letter addressed to her before, let alone one that looked as exciting as this. She turned the envelope over and examined the mask stamped into the purple wax seal. Her heart skipped.

'Go on, open it!' Seffie urged, bouncing up and down. There was a gleam in her eyes.

Eagerly, Aribella prised open the seal and read the card inside:

Dear Aribella,

You are cordially invited to your mask fitting.

Please be prompt.

Tardiness is not tolerated.

Distinti saluti,

The Mask Maker

Aribella's stomach swooped with joy. She couldn't believe it. She was getting a mask, a mask made just for her. A mask that would make her unwatchable and help her control her power and breathe underwater, and so many other marvellous things.

She read the letter again and frowned. 'It doesn't say when the fitting is.'

'That's because it's now,' Rosa announced cheerily. 'Are you ready to go?'

13

'Wh-what?' Aribella didn't feel at all prepared to have the fitting right this minute.

'He's like that, I'm afraid, sweetie.' Rosa turned the corners of her mouth down apologetically. 'Oh, don't look so worried, you'll be fine. Rodolfo said he'd take you. Do you have your room key there? You have to hand it in whenever you leave the hotel, remember.'

Aribella nodded, dimly recalling that this was one of the rules from Rosa's list. She pulled the heavy gold key out of her pocket. At least it meant she wouldn't lose it.

Rosa took the key and hung it back on a hook. Her fingers lingered on it for a moment, as they had when she'd first selected it, and Aribella wondered if there was something about the room that was bothering her.

Rodolfo emerged from the lounge with a tension to his jaw.

'Good news,' he said, though he didn't seem to fully believe this. 'I'm to have an audience with the Doge at the end of next week, so I can ask about your papa then.'

'Next week?' Aribella was unable to hide her disappointment. A week was too long for Papa to spend alone in a prison cell.

'I'm sorry, Aribella, I really am. If it was up to me . . .' Rodolfo shook his head. 'But it's the best that can be done for the time being. The Elders are very firm on Inbellis matters. Everything must be done the proper way.'

'Rodolfo did all he could,' Rosa added. 'Honestly, Aribella. A week isn't that long – relatively speaking,' she added quickly, seeing Aribella's mouth opening to protest.

Aribella fell silent, trying to quell her frustration. She felt so guilty for being in this luxurious hotel, receiving gifts, when he was locked up.

'We're going to get him out,' Rodolfo said firmly. 'That's the main thing. For now, try to put it from your mind. Concentrate on your fitting. I will take care of your papa.'

Aribella knew it was good advice. Maybe once she got her mask she could sneak into the prison to visit Papa. She could even take him some pastries.

'Jacapo has suggested I take her, Rodolfo,' said Ursula, appearing from the lounge behind him. 'He says you've got enough on your plate, what with all the star readings.'

Rodolfo frowned. 'Surely you need to rest, Ursula? You're the one who fainted.'

'Oh, I was just a little shocked. Don't know what came over me. Always been a little . . . squeamish. Anyway, the fresh air will do me good and I'd love to get to know our new guest.' Ursula smiled brightly. Her pale blue gown matched her eyes. It had a white fur collar that Seffie was staring at angrily.

As Aribella met Ursula's gaze, she felt a nudging in her head. It was an unsettling sensation, as if someone was poking around in her mind.

'Oh, you're so worried about your papa,' Ursula said. 'But you mustn't be. Rodolfo will soon make sure he's safe.'

Aribella blinked in surprise. How had Ursula known? Was it that obvious?

'And Seffie, you can stop wishing me death threats over the fur – it's an heirloom.'

Rosa frowned. 'Ursula, you're not supposed to read the minds of Novices without their permission . . .'

So that explained the nudging feeling. Ursula was a mind-reader.

'Sorry, sorry. A bad habit.' Ursula turned to Rodolfo and the nudging stopped.

Rodolfo laughed. 'I'd appreciate it if you didn't try to read my mind either, Ursula.'

'If only I could. I might have stopped you getting in trouble last night. But you've always been good at blocking me, Rodolfo.' Ursula sighed and turned to check her hair in a mirror.

'It's not as easy now I'm getting older.'

'Aren't we all?' Ursula gazed at her reflection and winced. 'Time is so cruel. Well, we'd better get a move on, Aribella. The Mask Maker values punctuality. And as he only sees people with an appointment, we don't want to risk missing your slot.'

Aribella hesitated. She wanted Rodolfo to take her, but Rodolfo did look tired and it was kind of Ursula to offer – just so long as she didn't try to read Aribella's mind again. Anyway, it didn't seem as if she had much of a choice.

'I'll meet you later,' Seffie whispered. 'Can't wait to see what mask you get.'

Aribella nodded, smiling nervously.

Ursula put on her mask at the entrance doors. It was a half-mask with a mirror-like surface and a series of rings that crossed at different angles and met at the centre of the forehead where there was a painted eye.

Aribella watched, carefully noting how Ursula tied the black ribbons, in case there was some knack to it that she might be tested on later.

'You'll have your own one soon enough,' Ursula said, pushing the doors open.

They stepped into the crisp autumn day. Ursula's heeled shoes clicked as she crossed the jetty to one of the striped mooring posts. Ropes were tied round the post, trailing into the water. Ursula grabbed hold of one rope, wrinkling her nose.

'I wish there was another way to do this,' she muttered. Then humming a tune Aribella half recognized, she tugged on the rope.

Instantly, the water below the post churned and a black gondola emerged. Aribella remembered how Rodolfo's gondola had sunk into the canal last night and thought at first that this gondola might be the same one. But while it had the same winged lion emblem painted on it, this gondola had both cushioned benches and an elegant-looking central cabin. Silver swirls were painted over its hull and there were pink cushions everywhere. The gondola shook off the last of the glittering water droplets and when it finally rested on the surface it was bone-dry.

Ursula laughed and Aribella realized that nudging feeling in her head was happening again. She blushed.

'Oh, don't be embarrassed. It's fun seeing it all again through your eyes. I remember when I first arrived at the Halfway. Everything was amazing for me then too. Age makes you so jaded . . . One of its many perils.' She sighed. 'Anyway, get in, get in!'

Aribella climbed aboard awkwardly. She decided not to use the cabin and opted instead for the front bench so she could get a good view and feel the air on her face.

Ursula untied the mooring rope and pushed the gondola away from the jetty. Aribella wondered if it would go as fast as Rodolfo's, but it quickly became obvious that wasn't going to happen.

The Grand Canal was busy, and although Ursula's mask made them unwatchable, they had to move slowly to avoid bumping other boats and giving the people on board a shock. The gondola bucked and jolted, as if it found the slow pace tedious.

Aribella's thoughts drifted between Papa and Theo. What were they both doing now? Were they thinking of her? As soon as she got the mask she'd visit them, she promised herself, Elders' permission or not. She glanced nervously back at Ursula, hoping she hadn't read this thought.

The gondola soon turned off the Grand Canal on to a smaller canal lined with colourful mask shops.

Aribella and Theo had once idled away an afternoon rowing past these shops, stopping to pick out their favourite masks from the jaunty arrangements in their windows, knowing they'd never even be able to afford even the ribbons. But here Aribella was now, about to get a beautiful mask of her own . . . A fresh bubble of excitement rose in her chest. She made a game of guessing which shop belonged to the Cannovacci Mask Maker. But while all the masks in the windows would have impressed Aribella yesterday, today they looked flat and plain compared with the masks she'd seen at the Halfway Hotel. Indeed, Ursula skulled past all these shops without giving them a second glance.

Instead, she headed directly towards another side canal. This one was so narrow that it seemed impossible the gondola would be able to turn on to it, but the elegant craft skimmed round the bend without pause or bump.

The canal was dark and cold, and there did not seem to be any shops here at all, just dingy houses with boarded-up windows. Perhaps Ursula had made a wrong turn? Remembering the Halfway's transformation, Aribella tried to reserve judgement. Maybe these houses changed too once you were inside. But it was hard to believe. The Halfway, though it had appeared dilapidated, had always had a charm that

Aribella had been drawn to. These houses just made her feel afraid.

Ursula stopped the gondola outside the most run-down house of all. The windows were painted black, and so was the door. Aribella noticed two grey ovals painted in the centre of the door, like eyeholes, and the symbol of the winged lion underneath.

'You have to go in alone,' Ursula said. 'I'll be here when you're done.'

Aribella nodded and swallowed. Ursula wouldn't need to read her mind to know she was dreading it. She tried to pull herself together, and stepped out of the gondola on to the jetty. Would she be asked to demonstrate her power? She hoped not, her fingers were still sore from this morning's mishap at breakfast. What if she tried to use it and it got out of control? What would the Mask Maker think if she accidentally burnt down his shop?

'You'll be fine,' Ursula said. 'Go on.'

Steeling herself, Aribella knocked tentatively.

There was no reply. She felt a flutter of both relief and disappointment. Maybe he wasn't in and she'd have to come back another day . . . She glanced back at Ursula, who just nodded and waved Aribella on.

Aribella took a deep breath, turned to the door again and pushed it open, blinking into the gloom beyond.

14

'Hello?' she called. The room inside was dimly lit and filled with incense. She stepped in and the door closed softly behind her. Aribella tried to keep her breathing steady. Slowly her eyes adjusted. Shelves covered the walls, filled with rows of masks. This display was nothing like the merry mess in the windows of other mask shops. These masks were propped up delicately on stands, carefully arranged, and each looked as exquisitely made as any at the Halfway. These were Cannovacci masks.

Aribella gazed up at a hundred silent faces in awe. On a lower shelf was a mask covered in butterfly wings. Next to it, another had a crown made from golden feathers that couldn't have come from any bird in Venice. The higher the shelf, the more extravagant and strange the masks became. On the top shelf, only just visible in the darkness, was a mask made of razor clams next to another with steel slits for eyes and a cruel grate over the mouth. Aribella shivered. What powers were connected to those masks? There was something eerie about the way the masks seemed to watch her. A bone-white beaked mask in the corner gave her a particularly odd feeling . . .

In the middle of the room was an age-spotted mirror. Its patina was almost entirely clouded. On the brass stand next to the mirror several odd-looking instruments had been laid out. Aribella was just about to examine them when she noticed that the wall behind the mirror wasn't really a wall but a black curtain.

Her first thought was that the Mask Maker must be on the other side. But as she moved over and pulled the heavy curtain back, she had another sensation. As if she'd seen the curtain before, in a dream perhaps . . . But that couldn't be right. On the other side was a small room that was entirely empty, except for an empty mask stand.

'No one is to go into the bonding area without permission,' boomed a voice.

Aribella dropped the curtain as if it were red-hot, spinning round to see the beaked white mask flying across the room. Her mind flashed back to the spectre and she nearly jumped out of her skin – then she saw that the mask had a cloaked body attached to it, a body that, until now, she'd mistaken for shadows.

'You're lucky there wasn't a mask in there,' the white-beaked man continued crossly, 'or you'd have ruined the whole process. A new mask must be seen by no one but its future wearer and the Mask Maker during the first hours of its creation.'

'I'm sorry,' Aribella stammered. 'I was just wondering where you were. I'm Aribella. You invited me.' She pulled her card out of her pocket defensively.

'Yes, yes. The new girl.' The Mask Maker waved one hand as if he was already bored. He barely looked at her. 'Tell me, girl, what do you think of my masks?'

Worried this was a test, Aribella hesitated, searching for the right word to sum up the strange mix of feelings the masks gave her, one that wouldn't offend the Mask Maker. What did she feel? Awe? Fear?

Thankfully, the Mask Maker seemed to think speechlessness an appropriate response. 'It's the finest collection there is,' he said proudly.

'Whose are they?'

'Mine now. They were once the masks of Cannovacci. But just as our bodies return to the star dust that formed us, all masks return to the Maker in the end.'

Aribella shivered. So, it wasn't a gallery, it was a

mausoleum. The thought made her feel strange, as if she was looking at the faces of the dead.

'Did you – did you make them all?'

'Of course not. How old do you think I am? Some of these masks are centuries old. They are the work of previous Mask Makers and their apprentices.'

'Who's your apprentice?' Aribella asked. Was it a Novice at the Halfway? she wondered. Or perhaps an Elder?

'I do not have one currently. The one I had . . . disappeared,' the Mask Maker said in a thin voice. 'Most . . . unfortunate,' he added, and Aribella got the unsettling feeling that his words brushed over some secret. He gave her a hard stare, almost as if he was seeing her for the first time then appeared to come to a decision. 'We must not waste time thinking of the past. What is done is done. Let us see what *you* can do.'

Without warning, the Mask Maker grabbed Aribella's arm. His fingers were like icicles, and it took everything Aribella had not to pull away, especially when he dragged her to the brass stand and picked up one of the strange-looking instruments. It was like a measuring compass, with two sharp prongs connected by a hinge. She tried not to wince as he placed the instrument against her forehead and adjusted it. The ends were sharp.

'Do not move.'

Aribella stayed absolutely still as he measured her forehead, the distance between her eyes, the length of her nose, mouth, ears . . . He even measured the distance between her nostrils, which made her want to sneeze. It was extremely difficult not to flinch, especially with the Mask Maker peering down his beak at her. After each measurement, he held the prongs against a ruler and noted the numbers in a small black notebook.

Finally, he snapped the instrument closed. 'Stand in front of the mirror.'

Aribella wondered what looking in the clouded glass would show the Mask Maker that he couldn't already see, but she did as he said.

As soon as she stepped before the mirror, however, the patina cleared and flames swirled where Aribella's reflection ought to be. Aribella tried to step away, but the Mask Maker held her shoulders firmly, watching intently as Aribella's outline appeared in the mirror beneath the flames. The flames reformed and centred around her hands, and a sudden feeling of warmth rose inside Aribella, dissolving all her doubts and fears. She felt powerful, strong. For a moment, she felt as if she was exactly where she belonged.

Then the Mask Maker pulled her away from the

mirror. The flames disappeared and the glass clouded over once more. Aribella tried to hold on to the edges of the feeling that had passed through her, but it ebbed as rapidly as it had arrived.

For the first time, the Mask Maker seemed excited. 'The mirror shows what's hidden inside us, an inner strength or perhaps a weakness that we're afraid to claim,' he explained. 'In your case it is a strength, a great strength. We have not had a fire Cannovacci for centuries. And so strong already . . .'

He started moving around the room, pulling boxes out from the bottom shelves that were full of all sorts of things: feathers, pieces of silk, buttons . . . and stranger things too. One box contained crystal monocles, another nothing but teeth. The Mask Maker held up a bronze disc and a dead beetle.

'It will be difficult to craft something good enough,' he continued, examining them, 'but there is nothing I love more than a challenge.'

Out of the corner of her eye, Aribella caught a flicker in the top corner of the room – way up on the highest shelf, like a bat or a bird fluttering its wings. Io? But it wasn't either of those things – it was something dark and curved. A mask. And it wasn't fluttering, it was falling now, hurtling past the shelves . . .

Aribella's hands opened. With an instinct that

surprised her, she caught it squarely between her palms. She'd barely moved at all: it was almost as if the mask hadn't fallen but *jumped* . . . But that couldn't be right.

The mask was full-faced yet incredibly light. A cloud of dust drifted away as Aribella turned it over to see the face. She recoiled instantly. It was hideously disfigured. There were deep gashes across either cheek, as though someone had deliberately cut into it, and a thin jagged line sliced across from top to bottom. It didn't look as though it belonged with the rest of the collection at all. Even the most frightening masks on the top shelves had a kind of beauty. This mask was just ugly.

'What are you doing? You're not to touch the masks!' The cold fury in the Mask Maker's voice made Aribella start. She looked up to see him glaring. He seemed even angrier than when he'd caught her looking behind the curtain.

'I didn't mean to. It fell.'

'Cannovacci masks never fall.'

It was Aribella's turn to glare. 'Of course masks fall . . . This one just did.' Why was he so angry with her? She'd just saved his mask from breaking. He should be thanking her.

She tried to hand the mask back but the Mask Maker recoiled. 'I don't know what trick you've used but if you can hold that mask it is now yours.'

'But I don't want it. Please take it back.'

'I can't. It is your mask now.'

This couldn't be happening. 'But it's not made for me. It won't work properly.' Not to mention the fact that it was ugly and horrible. 'I want a proper one,' she whispered pathetically. How had she messed this up?

'It makes no difference what you want. Turn the mask over and read the name inside.'

Aribella did as the Mask Maker said and her stomach dropped. Inside the grey lining a name was being scratched out, already illegible, but above it, in fresh golden writing, another appeared: *Aribella*.

Aribella had the sudden, sickening feeling that she was going to cry. She'd been so excited about getting a beautiful mask, one that she could be proud of, like Seffie's. A mask that *belonged* to her, that would make her fit in at the Halfway and let her sneak off to visit Papa and Theo. This ugly second-hand mask wouldn't do. And what if it didn't work?

'Please,' she begged. 'I need one like everyone else's.'

The Mask Maker looked at her squarely. 'Yes, I saw that in the mirror – that desperation to fit in. Tell me, why are you so determined to be like everyone else when what makes you different is your strength? True

130

power comes when we let go of false masks and accept ourselves as we truly are.'

And with that, the Mask Maker shoved Aribella out his shop and slammed the door.

The sunlight was harsh and blinding after the gloom.

'Mask Maker,' Ursula called out, hurrying up the jetty. 'I wondered if I could ask—?' She pushed the door but it did not budge. 'Oh dear, I suppose not . . . Why do you look so sad, Aribella?'

'It's nothing,' Aribella said firmly. But when she looked up at Ursula's beautiful mask she could feel hot tears springing to her eyes.

She jumped into the gondola and hid inside the cabin, shoving the hideous mask under a cushion. What would she tell Seffie when she asked about the mask? Aribella never wanted to show it to anyone. It felt like a symbol of her failure, her inability to fit in – even in a hotel full of misfits. If she didn't belong with them, then where did that leave her?

Aribella suddenly felt so lonely. She longed to confide in someone – someone who really knew her, who could understand and comfort her. But who could she talk to? Papa was in prison, and it had been a long time since he'd been able to comfort her anyway. Her best friend Theo probably feared her now. Rodolfo and Rosa still felt like strangers, and while Seffie was kind, she probably wouldn't want to be Aribella's friend when she saw the mask.

No, Aribella knew whom her soul longed for. It was the deepest and most painful longing of all, one she had tried always to suppress for fear of getting lost in it and drowning. But now, as Ursula rowed them quietly back to the Halfway – kindly not asking questions or reading her mind – Aribella allowed herself to long for her mama.

15

The following week passed surprisingly quickly. Aribella had expected it to drag but, despite all her worries over Papa and her hideous mask, she enjoyed her time at the Halfway. It was hard not to, when she ate pastries for breakfast and clam spaghetti for dinner, slept on feather pillows and silk sheets at night, and had friends like Seffie who was the best company Aribella could have asked for. Rosa had returned her old clothes – cleanly laundered, mended and folded – but Aribella couldn't face wearing them around the elegant hotel so had shoved them deep in the back of her wardrobe and chose a new dress every day.

The one part of hotel life Aribella dreaded was her training.

Following her disastrous fitting, she'd arrived back at the Halfway to discover that a new training room had appeared on the second floor with a fire symbol on the door and steel, flame-retardant walls inside. This was temporarily exciting, until Aribella discovered that her new mask was not only ugly and embarrassing but did not seem to help control her power at all. Seffie and Fin had both been very kind when they'd seen the mask but she could tell they'd been shocked; Seffie's feathery mask was so beautiful, while Fin's – a vivid fuchsia mask, with opals and amethysts swirling across the cheeks, and a headdress of gold leaf – was gloriously bright. Rodolfo had also seemed surprised but insisted that it would work, and offered to help with her training.

'It is still a Cannovacci mask,' he repeated during her sessions, as Aribella tried and failed once more to make the flames appear on command. 'It is your mask.'

'The Mask Maker didn't *give* it to me,' Aribella repeated. 'I told you, it fell. He didn't seem happy about it.'

'It is still yours.'

'Because of my name inside it?'

'Not just that. Here.' Rodolfo took off his starry mask and held it out to her. 'Try to take it.'

Aribella stared at the beautiful mask and felt

strangely reluctant. She thought she was just being silly until she reached out and touched it.

'Ouch!' It was as if she had been stung by a bee.

'Sorry, it was just easier to show you than to explain.'

'You could have tried explaining first!'

'Now, imagine trying to wear my mask. There's no way you could without your entire face blistering. So you see, if you can wear that mask then it's yours. Now let go of your doubts and *believe*.'

She often left training feeling worse than when she started.

At night, she rubbed a balm Marquesa had given her into her sore fingers. They seemed to be constantly in pain these days for, while the power wouldn't come when she wanted it to in training, it still came when she *didn't* want it to – twice during breakfast, once setting the edge of Rodolfo's star cloak alight, once when she was having a nightmare about the spectre – and it *hurt*. Rosa left buckets of water beside her bed and said it didn't matter but, as Aribella bundled up the singed sheets and tablecloths, she felt ashamed.

News reached the Halfway that the Doge's health had taken another turn for the worst, and he was missing more State occasions than ever. Aribella desperately hoped for his recovery and that his illness wouldn't mean Rodolfo couldn't meet him to discuss

Papa's release. It should be any day now.

Not only that, the water was higher than ever and the banks of the Grand Canal were overflowing. Whole sections of the city were now underwater, according to Seffie who had been brought news by the birds. Could it be connected to what had happened at the blood moon? There had been no more news of spectres and that was a relief. Still, she worried about Theo constantly: was he all right? Did he miss her? Was Gian being kinder to him now she was no longer there? She'd looked out of her window every morning since she'd arrived at the Halfway, but she hadn't seen his papa's boat yet. Aribella wondered if the fishing families were still struggling to catch fish.

She was distracted from her worries by Seffie, who wanted to play endless games of hide-and-seek. Fin would join in whenever he wasn't in the reading room, and sometimes Julietta and Bruno would play too, although they were a little older so mostly spent time with each other. Fin liked hide-and-seek as his ability to walk through walls made him hard to beat, but Seffie would often get Nymeria or Io to tell her where he had gone. Helena would sometimes catch Fin appearing through a wall, or Seffie growling at Nymeria, and threaten to tell the Elders, though she never actually did. Aribella still had no idea what Helena's power really was. Fin said he thought it was something to do with mind control, while Seffie swore it was just 'being annoying'.

The night before Rodolfo's meeting with the Doge Aribella fell into a fitful sleep and dreamt about the curtain at the Mask Maker's shop. In the dream, it billowed ahead of her, drawing her to it. A sound was coming from the other side, a voice . . . Was it Theo's? Someone was calling her name. She was just about to wrench the curtain back when something woke her. Luna was pawing her face.

The cat had been returning to Aribella's room most evenings via the balcony, and Aribella was grateful for the reminder of Burano. 'Ouch, get off, you silly thing.' She reached up to pull the cat into her arms, but Luna jumped off the bed and started to paw at the window.

Foggy-headed, Aribella crawled out of bed. Luna didn't usually ask to be let out until Aribella went down to breakfast. It was very early still, and the light outside was grey.

'What is it?' she asked, expecting to see a mouse or bird on her balcony. But there was nothing. 'Why have you woken me so early?'

Luna meowed.

Curious, Aribella pulled open the glass doors, shivering as the cold air froze her bare toes. She was about to retreat back inside and fetch her slippers when she heard a swish of oars and a voice she recognized.

'Theo, we've been over this.'

Theo and his papa!

Nervously, Aribella hugged her arms round herself and crept to the balcony's edge, knowing the hotel would make her unwatchable. Luna followed her, curling around Aribella's cold feet, warming them. Aribella ducked down and peered between the railings. Her heart leapt – there he was! Standing on his papa's boat, looking the same as always, his scruffy clothes flapping in the breeze, his curly hair flopping messily into his eyes. How good it was to see him! She wanted to shout out a greeting. But was she allowed? What would she say? And if Theo looked up, it would be like hearing a ghost. It was safer to keep quiet, though it hurt to do so.

Theo seemed uncharacteristically agitated. There weren't many other boats around at this time so his words carried clearly. It didn't take her long to realize, with a small tug on her heart, that he was talking about her.

'You don't really believe all they're saying, do you? We're still struggling to catch fish and now we're getting this flooding too. If Aribella was the cause—'

'Don't know, son. Some folk think the water's going down.'

'Well, it's not. And the fish are still gone. If Aribella was the reason, and she's been put in prison, how do you explain that?'

'I don't know, Theo. But there's lots being said about what she did at the market.'

Aribella felt a flush of shame. Her fingers tingled and she quickly clenched her fists. Luna pressed herself closer to Aribella's feet.

'You think she's a witch, don't you, Pa? You're just a superstitious sucker like the rest of them.'

'Watch your tongue, and keep your voice down. I don't know what I think.'

'Well, I do. She's my friend.'

Their boat drifted under the Rialto Bridge and the rest of Theo's words were lost. The Grand Canal was empty again. Aribella felt empty too. Even though she knew she should have anticipated Theo's papa's words, they still felt like blows. He'd always been so kind. Now it seemed he distrusted her too, like all the other fishing folk.

And poor loyal Theo thought she was locked up and suffering. It wasn't fair on him. She had to let him know she was all right. She looked back into her bedroom and her gaze fell upon the empty eyes of her hideous mask. There was no more time to waste on doubts.

Second-hand and ugly or not, she was going to make it work.

16

Aribella dressed quickly and slipped out into the corridor. There was still an hour before breakfast and the hotel was quiet, apart from the faint swish of oars on canals, and snores coming from behind bedroom doors. There was some odd quality to the quiet, but she couldn't put her finger on what it was.

She hurried down to her fireproof training room on the second floor, crept in and closed the door softly. She put on the mask and tied the ribbons. As usual, it felt hot and uncomfortable. Her warped reflection looked back at her in the four steel walls. She immediately felt as hopeless as always. But then she thought of Theo and Papa, and knew she had to keep trying.

She thought of all Rodolfo had taught her and all that the Mask Maker had said. She remembered the warm feeling she'd had looking in the mirror at the Mask Maker's shop. She met her own gaze and tried to summon this feeling once more. She tried to think of the good fire could do – that it could cook and warm and guide someone home on a dark night. She tried to *like* her power, to understand that it was hers and hers alone. At first, her attempts felt useless, but then – as she practised – a surge of heat thrummed through her. It was not the sudden snap of heat that heralded the flames but a warm glow that spread down her arms and into her hands, making her feel powerful and strong.

Her fingers started to tingle and she looked down at her hands. A surge of pure joy went through her. Flames danced across both her palms, as they had in the shop – only this time they weren't just in her reflection. This was real. There was no pain, no fear. Instead, the flames felt like old friends – familiar, as if they were part of her and always had been.

Aribella had no idea how long she stayed there, holding fire in her palms: it could have been minutes or hours. Eventually she closed her hands and the flames extinguished. She stepped back, panting. Her fingers did not hurt . . . She'd done it. She'd actually done it! She'd summoned her power.

The mask vibrated against her skin, almost happily,

as if it was purring.

Triumphantly, Aribella untied the ribbons of the mask and pulled it off more carefully than usual, no longer detesting it as much. She turned the mask over and looked at the scratched-out name under her own, trying to work out what it said, but it was no good. She looked at her own name. It didn't matter whose mask this had been, it was hers now, she told herself, starting to believe it could be true.

When she crept back out into the hallway, she was met by the delicious smell of cooked garlic and heard the murmur of voices coming from the floor below. She realized everyone must be in the dining room for lunch. Was it that late already? With a rumbling tummy, and still reeling from her success, Aribella hurried towards the stairs. She couldn't wait to tell Seffie and Fin about her morning.

A voice from behind one of the training doors made her stop.

'Almost . . .' It was Helena's voice.

The door was ajar. Aribella peeped through. Helena must have decided to put in some extra practice too.

The room had been set up like a classroom, with a blackboard, chairs and desks, and four clocks, one on each wall. Helena was watching one of the clocks. Her spiky hair stuck up behind a full-faced copper mask that was covered in hundreds of small cogs. She did not seem to be doing anything at all.

For several minutes, Aribella watched as Helena remained in the same position, still staring at the hands of the clock. Aribella started to get bored, until she noticed that a vase of flowers had moved from one end of the room to the other. She blinked. The next second a line of writing appeared on the blackboard. Had Helena done that? Fin thought her power was connected to mind control. Maybe she had the same power as Rosa and could make things appear out of nowhere. But why would she hide that? Wait. Now Helena was at the other end of the room. How had that happened? Julietta was the one with speed.

The next second Helena appeared by the door . . .

Quickly, Aribella ducked behind a large statue. It was a tight squeeze, and something sharp dug into her shoulder. A portrait frame was sharing her hiding place.

She waited, heart racing, until Helena had passed safely by and her footsteps had faded. Then she shuffled out, and turned back to pull out the portrait. The subject was a lady with long dark hair, wearing a green dress that matched her eyes. Her glittering mask was covered in flowers, birds and silver fish. The plaque underneath read: *Clara.*

Aribella started, remembering the conversation between Rodolfo and Jacapo in the lounge that first morning. Clara! So this was Zio's murderer. That explained why her portrait had been removed from the walls. Why hadn't it been destroyed though?

Hearing more footsteps, Aribella slid the portrait back into its hiding place, and hurried to the dining room.

She found Seffie and Fin at a table of their own. Bruno and Julietta were sitting together on another table. Helena was nowhere to be seen. Some of the Elders were there – Ursula, Marquesa – but Rodolfo was absent. She hurried across to the buffet table and helped herself to a large plate of risotto.

Seffie raised an eyebrow at Aribella as she sat down. 'Where've you been?'

'Practising,' she replied. Between mouthfuls of hot, creamy risotto, she told them about her morning.

'Well done, Aribella!' Fin said, clapping her on the back and looking impressed.

'Yes, well done, Ari,' Seffie agreed. But she seemed distracted and not nearly as happy about her news as Aribella had expected her to be. Aribella gave Fin an enquiring look.

Fin just shrugged. 'Dessert fixes most things. Back in

a minute.' He went to the buffet table.

'Seffie, what's wrong?' Aribella asked gently.

Seffie's lip trembled. 'It's the birds!' she said, bursting into tears. 'They've g-gone.'

'What? Where?'

'I don't know,' Seffie wailed. 'They didn't tell me. They didn't even say goodbye! This morning, I tried to call to some of them on the roof but none replied. I've looked for them everywhere but all their nests are empty. They've just vanished.'

Aribella thought back to the odd quietness this morning and suddenly understood what had been missing. There'd been no birdsong.

Fin returned to their table and passed round three generous slices of cherry tart.

'I heard Theo on the Grand Canal this morning,' Aribella said. 'He says the flooding is getting worse.'

Seffie rubbed her eyes. 'Even during *acqua alta* it's not this bad.'

'It's strange that the fish have gone too.'

Seffie sat up. 'Really?'

Aribella nodded. 'They've been scarce for months.'

'Do you think it's connected?' Fin asked thoughtfully, his spoonful of tart paused in mid-air.

'It could be. I don't know . . .' Aribella admitted. But she had a very bad feeling. 'What about the blood moon?' she said hesitantly.

Silence followed her words.

'Rodolfo said that the blood moon signalled that the boundary between the worlds of living and the dead is weak,' she went on.

She had told Seffie and Fin what had happened to her, and what had been said in that first meeting with the Elders. But as nothing further had happened on the lagoon, the Elders seemed to have relaxed. Was that a mistake?

'The books in the reading room might be useful,' Fin mused. 'I'll check.' He got up and left, still clutching his spoon of uneaten tart.

Aribella and Seffie hadn't touched their tarts either.

'Should we tell the Elders?' Aribella whispered, glancing towards their table. 'Do you think they know already?'

'We should talk to Rodolfo,' said Seffie. 'He's the only one who seems to care.'

'He might have seen something about it in the stars too,' Aribella agreed. 'In any case, we have to warn the islanders that the lagoon might not be safe. And if the flooding continues the whole of Venice will soon be underwater – Burano too.'

Aribella and Seffie headed to the roof to find Rodolfo. However, as they reached the landing of the third floor they heard voices from the landing above. It was Jacapo and Rodolfo.

'How many times must I remind you that it is forbidden to interfere in the affairs in the Inbellis without approval of the council, Rodolfo?' boomed Jacapo.

'I'm not a Novice, Jacapo,' Rodolfo replied, 'so please do not talk to me like one.'

'I'll stop talking to you like a Novice when you stop acting like one.'

'What difference does it really make if I visit the poor man or not, Jacapo? I'm assuming you know because of Ursula,' Rodolfo went on, 'which accounts for the awful headaches I've been having lately. Isn't *that* against Cannovacci rules?'

'She's acting in everyone's best interests, Rodolfo—'

' "Everyone" being who exactly?'

'Venice, of course.'

'Venice's best interests?' Rodolfo spat, and for the first time it sounded like he was losing his temper. 'An innocent man is in prison, alone and afraid, and you will do nothing to help. The water is rising and you continue to ignore it. There is a spectre on the lagoon, a spectre that attacked an islander and a Novice, and you ignore that too. And this morning there are no birds – and still you act as if nothing is wrong. Our duty is to protect Venice – Cannovacci,

Inbellis and animals included. Not to hide in a palazzo with our heads in the sand.'

'We are meant to maintain an appropriate distance.'

'The boundary between worlds is under threat – when will you start listening? Another blood moon is coming, Jacapo. Soon. I have seen it. And when it does, the Island of the Dead will rise and darkness will come for us all unless someone stops it.'

'We have just had a blood moon and there was no darkness, just one spectre, or so you and your new Novice would have us believe—'

'Just one that night,' Rodolfo cut in. 'But the next time there could be hundreds.'

'Hundreds? Come on, Rodolfo,' Jacapo said. 'The boundary can't be destroyed to that degree. Who would be capable of that?'

'You both know who I think is behind this,' Rodolfo replied coolly.

'I will not have any more of this slander. Zio was murdered!'' Jacapo roared. 'By Clara!'

'The evidence is not conclusive—'

'That is enough. It's time you put the Cannovacci first, Rodolfo.' Jacapo's voice shook with fury. 'You are breaking the sacred oath. I shall call an emergency meeting of the Elders to see that you are forbidden from leaving the hotel, and if you disobey I shall suggest you are checked-out from Halfway and your mask seized!'

Aribella's stomach dropped. Next to her, Seffie cursed quietly.

'You cannot leave Venice so vulnerable.' Rodolfo's voice had risen.

'I'm *protecting* Venice. From you! Your lack of judgement may cause the city and the Cannovacci great harm. It is clear we can no longer trust you. If you leave the hotel again, I will see to it that you are checked-out before tomorrow.'

Heavy footsteps stomped down the stairs towards Aribella and Seffie. They quickly hid round the corner as Jacapo strode past, more red-faced than ever.

Once he had disappeared, Aribella and Seffie hurried upstairs and found Rodolfo still on the landing, deep in thought.

'Rodolfo,' Aribella called.

He blinked as if coming back to the present. 'Aribella, Seffie, why are you—?'

'We heard everything,' Aribella blurted. 'Can you really not visit the Doge?'

Rodolfo shook his head grimly. 'Jacapo will have the rule of the council behind him. He'll be seeing to that now.' His blue eyes were full of apology. 'I'm sorry, Aribella.'

'Can't you just make yourself unwatchable and go anyway?' said Seffie.

Rodolfo shook his head. 'Not now. I can't risk losing my mask. I need to read the stars more than ever.'

Aribella swallowed the lump in her throat and shook her head. 'It's my fault. I asked you to help.' Tears of frustration sprang to her eyes.

Rodolfo looked back at her so kindly. His eyes were shining strangely. 'I wish I could think of a way to send someone to the palace in my place,' he murmured, 'but no other Elders will go. I've always thought younger voices were better heard anyway. And I've always given permission for anyone to take my gondola as long as their intentions are good. Maybe that person, or *persons*,' he added pointedly, looking from Aribella to Seffie, 'could inform the Doge about the possible dangers on the lagoon too, so that he could warn the Inbellis islanders not to be on the lagoon at night . . . Here.'

He reached into the pocket of his cloak and pulled out a tiny wooden gondola, no bigger than his palm. He handed it to Aribella.

'What's this?' Aribella asked, looking down at the beautiful little craft. It was an exact replica of Rodolfo's gondola in miniature. Every detail was perfect, from the *ferro* to the oarlock, from the threadbare cushions to the symbol of the winged lion on its hull.

Seffie's eyes were wide. 'It's his *permesso*. It means you can use his gondola. But Signore, I thought Novices weren't allowed to use the gondolas?'

'Since when have *you* cared for rules, Persephone?' Rodolfo said. 'Sometimes they must be broken, if the reason is important enough.' He sighed and looked at Aribella intently. 'Please believe that whatever happens, you must trust me. And above all, trust yourself.'

'What's that mean?' Seffie whispered, as Rodolfo turned away, heading towards the roof.

'I don't know,' Aribella frowned. 'Do you think Jacapo will really exile Rodolfo from the hotel?'

Seffie shook her head. 'Let's hope Rodolfo can persuade the other Elders to support him.' She nodded towards the little gondola Aribella held in her hands. 'But right now, we've got a journey to make. Let's go!'

17

'It's all very well Rodolfo giving us his *permesso*,' Seffie puffed, pulling the mooring rope, 'but what use is that if he doesn't tell us how to get the gondola out of the canal?'

Aribella rubbed her mask to hide her own frustration. It was hot and annoying but she didn't dare remove it in case it made her visible to passing barges. They'd been out on the jetty for ages, taking it in turns to tug on Rodolfo's mooring rope, while the other person watched the windows, in case an Elder looked out. Luna was lying near the hotel entrance, one eye open.

'Oh, lovely rope,' said Seffie, 'please, please, pretty please – MOVE!' She heaved, but nothing happened and she lost her grip, almost tumbling into the canal.

'That's it. I'm getting Bruno. If he can't pull the gondola out, no one can.'

'No, Seffie, the fewer people who know the better,' Aribella said. 'I don't think it's about strength. Ursula didn't have to try very hard. There must be something else we're meant to do . . .' There was a sound like a pair of leather gloves flapping and a small black shape flitted across her vision. Io landed on the mooring post, curling his wings round his little body.

'Io!' Seffie exclaimed happily. 'Rodolfo must have sent him to help us.' She started making clicking sounds. To Aribella, she explained, 'Bats make sounds that are two or three times higher than humans can hear, so all you'll hear is clicks. It's really difficult to master and I'm not quite there yet, but hopefully I can understand.'

Io made a few quiet clicks, and Seffie frowned.

'What is it? What did he say?' asked Aribella impatiently.

'I don't understand. It sounds like he's . . . but he can't be.' Seffie shook her head.

'What?' Aribella pressed, feeling left out.

'It sounds like he's . . . singing or something. Do you think he's winding us up?'

Io made a few more clicking sounds.

'Of course!' Aribella picked up the slimy rope and

hummed the same tune Ursula had sung when she took her to the Mask Maker, all the time tugging gently.

'Not you too,' Seffie groaned. 'What is this about?'

But the next second, Seffie's protests died in her throat, for a curved *ferro* emerged from the canal water, followed by the body of a sleek black gondola, shaking water from its hull. The winged golden lion painted on its side gleamed.

'You did it, Ari!' Seffie squealed, slapping Aribella on the back.

Aribella glanced up at the Halfway's windows. No one was watching. Eager not to waste more time, she untied the rope and they jumped in. A thrum of excitement filled her chest as she stood on the crescent-shaped stern. She pocketed the *permesso* and took up the heavy oar. Its wood was smooth and slippery. She gripped it tightly, afraid it would slide right out of her grasp. Her fingers tingled and she felt excitement rush up inside her. She had never been allowed to steer *any* boat before, let alone a gondola.

Theo would be so impressed . . . and envious.

Io settled on the *ferro*, apparently coming with them. Aribella was pleased. They could use all the help they could get. Luna stayed where she was on the jetty, both eyes open now.

'To the palace,' Seffie called.

Aribella lifted the oar into the lock. It took a few attempts – Aribella teetering as she tried to keep her balance – but finally, after some jimmying, the oar slid into position. It then took a few tries to get the boat moving. On her first stroke, the oar came crashing out on to the deck.

'Sorry, Sef!' She shoved both her mask and the oar back into place, and threw all her weight into the next stroke. This time the wrong part of the blade hit the water and a curtain of spray showered them both.

'Gentler, Ari,' Seffie whispered. 'Gondolas are like animals. You have to be kind.'

Aribella did as Seffie suggested and held the oar as if she was holding Luna, without gripping or fear. The feeling she'd had that morning in training came rushing back to her and she felt the hull of the gondola vibrate and her mask tingle, both of them responding to her.

The oar slipped easily through the water and the gondola slid forwards.

Seffie cheered and soon they were skimming along the Grand Canal as if Aribella had been rowing gondolas her whole life. It felt amazing to be good at something so instantly, almost as if she'd been born to do it, and very quickly they reached the Palace entrance. She had been scared her mask wouldn't work outside the hotel, but Seffie had no such worries and they floated past the guards unseen and moored among the palace gondolas, which, on closer inspection, weren't half as impressive as the Halfway's.

Unwatchable, they crept up the stone steps and into an inner courtyard. An enormous marble staircase led up to the floor above, flanked by two male statues at the top. One man held a fish, and the other a very sharp-looking spear. Aribella gazed up at them, allowing herself a moment to marvel that she was here, inside the palace of the Doge. Her mask was still tingling.

'The Giants' Staircase,' Seffie whispered. 'Those two are Neptune and Mars, representing Venice's history of sea and war . . . What?' she added quickly, when Aribella shot her a look. 'Sometimes I listen when Fin's talking. Race you!'

Aribella followed her as quietly as she could. At the top of the staircase was a set of oak doors. Seffie turned the heavy iron handles and the door screeched. A long corridor extended in both directions.

'Where do you think the Doge is?' Aribella asked, looking around, but Io was already fluttering down the corridor, leading the way.

Aribella and Seffie hurried after the little bat,

occasionally losing sight of him in the shadows, only to spot him again ahead. The long corridor was full of statues, ornaments, drapes and dark paintings. It smelt of lemon and dust.

Aribella was glad Io was here to lead the way. The palace was like a maze.

Her mask wasn't tingling any more – it was *stinging* her, not quite as badly as Rodolfo's had when she'd tried to take it from him. But strong enough to make her untie the ribbons and pull it off.

'What's the matter, Ari?' Seffie whispered, pulling off her own mask in concern.

What was going on? Was the mask only now deciding that she wasn't its owner after all? But no, her name was still there, written inside it. Except . . . was that her imagination or did the letters beneath it look less crossed out?

'My mask – it stung me,' she managed before a voice barked from behind them.

'What are you two doing in here? How did you get in?'

Aribella looked up, full of panic. Three guards were approaching. Quickly she shoved the mask into the pocket of her clock.

'Please,' she said desperately, 'we have an appointment with the Doge. Our master sent us in his place.'

The guards looked at them sceptically, and one said gruffly, 'We'll soon see about that.'

'A likely story,' another scoffed.

'It's the truth!' Seffie said fiercely.

'Then why did you not announce yourselves at the gate? Come on, we're taking you for questioning.' He grabbed Aribella's arm. Her fingers itched and it took all her concentration to stop her power rising up inside her.

She heard doors opening at the end of the corridor.

'What is the meaning of all this?' said a thin voice.

Aribella spun round and saw a glittering mask and snow-white robes. Her breath caught.

The Doge of Venice!

18

t once, the guards bowed.

'We just found these two sneaking around the palace, Serenissimo Principe,' said the first guard, who was still holding Aribella tightly. 'They claim they're here to see you. But we've no idea how they got in.' He glared at one of his companions, who must have been on guard duty.

'We've come on behalf of Signore Rodolfo Foscari, Serenissimo Principe,' Aribella burst out, before the guard could silence her. 'About one of your prisoners. A lacemaker from Burano.'

'On behalf of Rodolfo, you say?' For a moment, the Doge remained unreadable, but then he opened his arms wide. 'Well, any friend of Rodolfo's is a friend of mine. Unhand my guests, please. Come, let us discuss this in my chamber.'

Aribella and Seffie, still flanked closely by the guards, followed the Doge through the doors into the most enormous room Aribella had ever seen, bigger even than those at the Halfway. The ceiling was as high as two houses and every inch of wall was covered with dark frescos in gilt frames. Even the ceiling had a fresco so vast and detailed it made Aribella's eyes water.

Searching for something to look at that wouldn't give her a headache, Aribella found her gaze drawn to the top border of the chamber walls, where there were faces painted. She recognized the distinctive cone-shaped crowns painted on their heads. Every Doge that had ever ruled Venice must be painted here, she realized, to watch over the Republic's affairs for ever. Aribella noticed a small, winged shape hanging upside down from the border. Io! She knew he could look after himself.

'Leave us,' the Doge said to his guards, who seemed reluctant but nevertheless obeyed. Seffie blew a very loud raspberry at the man who'd been holding her, and Aribella's body sagged with relief. She rubbed her sore arms. Soon it was just the Doge, Aribella, Seffie and, in the top corner, Io.

'Forgive the hostility,' the Doge said kindly in his thin voice. 'My guards are just being protective. But they don't know about the Cannovacci or their wonderful masks.' He gazed appreciatively at Seffie's beautiful animal mask, before tapping his own with a gloved finger. It was encrusted with so many diamonds that it sparkled wonderfully in the lamp-light, but still looked oddly flat and plain compared to the Cannovacci masks. 'I'm an admirer, you see . . . Do you have one too?' he asked Aribella.

Aribella didn't know what to do. She hated her horrid mask and didn't want to show it to such an important man. Neither did she want the mask to hurt him as it had just hurt her.

'No . . .' she lied, feeling the heat of it in her pocket. 'Not yet.' She felt Seffie glance at her, but said nothing. Aribella knew her friend understood how embarrassed she was of her mask.

'Look more at mine,' Seffie cut in, partly to help Aribella. She held up her mask and the Doge leant in to look curiously. Aribella could see his pale blue eyes through his mask.

'Wonderful,' he said, but he sounded disappointed – or possibly confused.

Aribella suspected he was being generous. She wondered how much the Doge really knew of the Cannovacci. She thought of the Lion's Mouth and suspected that the Cannovacci shared with the Doge only as much as they had to. Still, it was a relief to hear he knew Rodolfo. It would make her plea for Papa a lot easier.

'And how is Rodolfo? I do hope he's not fallen ill as well.' The Doge coughed. 'Terrible thing, old age. Just terrible.'

'Oh no, he's—' Aribella stopped. It was probably best the Doge didn't find out that Rodolfo was currently banned from coming to the palace. 'He just thought it would be better to send me, seeing as I'm the daughter of the prisoner.'

'Daughter? You mean, you have a parent in my prison?'

Aribella nodded. 'Yes, my father – and he's not well, Signore— I mean, Serenissimo Principe.' She blushed.

'Oh, Signore is fine, dear girl.'

'Thank you, Seren— Signore. My papa was accused of witchcraft, but it wasn't him, you see . . .'

'It was you.' The Doge nodded. 'I understand. And of course you are no witch. I will rectify this as quickly as I can.'

'You'll release him?'

'As soon as possible. Though like you Cannovacci, I am also bound by certain rules. There are proper codes of conduct I must follow. But I can ensure that his trial is brought forward and I promise you it will be fair.'

Aribella had hoped for Papa's release, but still she felt a surge of gratitude towards the kindly Doge. 'Really?'

'Of course. After all, the Cannovacci keep our city safe. It's the least I can do. And until the trial, I will see to it that he is well looked after.'

'Oh, thank you, Signore, thank you!' She looked at Seffie, who was also beaming.

She heard Io click and Seffie nudged her. Aribella remembered what Rodolfo had said.

'Signore, there's something else. We think there's something . . . evil, out on the lagoon. A creature. Or creatures,' she added, unsure how much the Doge would understand if she started talking about the spectre. 'They are very dangerous. Please warn the fishermen not to fish after dark and all the islanders to stay off the lagoon at night.'

The Doge nodded. 'My guards already patrol the lagoon. I am sure that if there is a danger, I will be the first to know. After all, we have the same goal – to protect Venice.'

It was such a relief to hear the Doge say this and Aribella felt a huge weight lift from her shoulders.

'However, I will make sure the islanders are aware of the dangers of fishing at night. Now, I think it's time you two got back to your hotel.' The Doge rang a small golden bell.

The doors opened and the guards reappeared.

'Guards, please escort my guests out. Goodbye, dear girls.'

The disgruntled guards led Aribella and Seffie back to the gondola, although this time without any painful arm-pinching. Behind them came the light flap of leathery wings. The guards blinked when they saw the gondola and Aribella was sure they were wondering how two children had got it into the palace right under their noses.

'What happened with your mask? Why did it hurt you?' Seffie asked, as the guards left them and they climbed aboard.

'I don't know,' Aribella admitted. 'I don't get it.'

'My mask will make us both unwatchable on the way back so you don't have to wear it if you don't want to.'

'Thanks, Seffie,' Aribella said, relieved about this – and the fact that her friend hadn't mentioned her lie to the Doge. Her face was still smarting.

As Seffie untied the mooring rope, she took up the oar and slipped it into the water. She was worried she might have trouble rowing without the mask and wondered if she should ask Seffie to row instead, but she had enjoyed the journey here so much that she found she was reluctant to give up the oar. She needn't have worried, however, for this time the oar responded instantly, as if the gondola recognized her, and they moved smoothly out on to the lagoon and back to the Grand Canal. Io wheeled away into the sky.

Despite her trouble with the mask, Aribella felt lighter. The Doge had proved as kind as she'd hoped. He was surely going to make sure Papa was freed, and to warn the islanders. For the first time since seeing the spectre, she did not feel so worried about the people she loved most. As she rowed back up the Grand Canal towards the Halfway Hotel, a bubble of happiness filled her chest.

That was until she saw Jacapo standing on the hotel's jetty, waiting for them.

19

J acapo's expression was thunderous. Behind him, Ursula was twisting her hands nervously.

Aribella and Seffie had no choice but to steer the gondola towards the jetty, jumped out and hurriedly tied the rope to the mooring post. As soon as it was secure, the gondola sank into the canal. Aribella wished she could disappear too.

'Where have you been?' Jacapo snapped. 'Who gave you a *permesso* to use that gondola?'

'I—' Aribella started. She didn't want to get Rodolfo into more trouble.

'We—' Seffie stammered.

'Ursula?' Jacapo said.

Aribella desperately tried to hide her thoughts, but it was no good. She felt Ursula's eyes boring into her.

The nudging feeling started in her head.

'They were at the palace,' Ursula said. 'Asking the Doge about Aribella's papa. Rodolfo gave them his *permesso.*'

If possible, Jacapo looked even more furious than before. 'You went to the palace? After everything I said to Rodolfo this morning! It's the final straw. He will lose his mask over this, I'll make sure of it!'

'I'm sorry, Signore,' Aribella gushed. 'I had to ask about Papa. It wasn't Rodolfo's fault, it was mine.'

'It was both of ours,' Seffie cut in. 'And we didn't just go for Aribella's papa. We needed to warn the Doge that something has made the birds and fish leave Venice, and that people should be careful on the lagoon. He was grateful we told him. He's going to make the guards patrol the lagoon, and warn people not to go out there at night.'

'I see Rodolfo has already filled your head with his silly theories!' Jacapo said. 'Venice is not in danger, if it was Nymeria would have alerted us.'

'But all Nymeria does is sleep,' said Seffie. 'How's she meant to alert anyone?'

The doors of the Halfway opened and Rosa rushed out on to the jetty. 'Jacapo, Ursula, please! May we do this inside? Passers-by may not be able to see you, but if you keep shouting they will hear you. We don't want them thinking there are ghosts on the Grand Canal.'

Jacapo's lips pursed, but he turned and marched through the doors. Ursula followed, avoiding their eyes. Rosa gestured to Aribella and Seffie, and they traipsed into the Halfway too.

'I'm sorry for getting you into trouble,' Aribella whispered to Seffie.

'Don't be silly,' Seffie whispered back. 'It was worth it.'

They smiled at each other.

'I think the only thing to do is to take their masks away until they learn to use them responsibly,' Jacapo said as soon as the doors were closed.

Seffie let out a cry of dismay, hugging her precious animal mask to her chest.

Aribella's stomach dropped. She hated her mask and it certainly wasn't working properly, but it was the only mask she had. How could she practise her power without it?

'Really, Jacapo!' Rosa interjected. 'They're Novices and this is their first offence. Aribella must have been very worried about her papa, though I know that's no excuse for rule-breaking,' she added quickly, as Jacapo's lips pursed again. 'But they deserve a second chance . . . Leave it with me. Rest assured, I will think of a suitably arduous chore to give them as punishment.'

Jacapo still looked livid, but he turned reluctantly to Aribella and Seffie and said, 'Fine. But I'm watching you two. Do anything else like this again and your masks will be taken quicker than you can both say "Grand Canal". Do you understand?'

Aribella and Seffie both nodded quickly.

Jacapo glared at them one last time before marching up the staircase. Ursula hurried after him.

'Phew,' Seffie blew her breath out loudly. 'Did you see how Ursula couldn't even look at us? Didn't realize she was such a coward. How dare she read our thoughts? She must be really trying to impress Jacapo . . . Thanks, Rosa. You really got us off the hook.'

But Rosa was not smiling. 'Don't look so relieved, Persephone. What you did was still against the rules and it has consequences.'

'We had Rodolfo's *permesso*,' Seffie muttered.

'Which reminds me, hand it over,' Rosa said.

Reluctantly, Aribella passed Rosa the miniature gondola. She felt awful for getting Rodolfo into trouble too, even though it had been his suggestion. She looked over at Nymeria. As always, the golden lioness was sleeping deeply. Did that really mean Venice was safe?

'Thank you. Anyway, my punishment won't be nearly as severe as Jacapo's would have been,' Rosa continued. 'As it happens, I need some help in the reading room, checking all the overdue book records. Fin's already volunteered.'

'Of course he has,' Seffie muttered.

'You two can help him every afternoon.'

'Until when?'

'Until it's done, Persephone.'

'But the reading room is huge!' Seffie protested.

'Well then, the sooner you get started the better,' Rosa said in a tone that was uncharacteristically strict. But as they turned to go up the staircase, she dropped her act for a moment to whisper, 'I hope you had good news about your father, by the way, Aribella?'

Aribella nodded, and some of the warm, bubbly feeling returned. Papa's release was definitely worth getting in trouble for. And how difficult could helping out in the reading room really be?

She soon found out.

20

'It will take us months to get through this,' Seffie complained.

They'd spent every afternoon that week in the reading room and had barely made a dent in the list of overdue books.

'And we're stuck doing it with Fin,' she groaned. 'I wish they'd just checked me out of Halfway.'

Aribella did not believe this at all. In truth, she suspected her wild-hearted friend had a secret soft spot for the bookish boy but covered it up by being mean about him. She'd seen lots of the fishing children do this with people they liked and had never understood why.

But Seffie was in a bad mood. She was missing her freedom and her birds. And to Aribella's dismay Luna had disappeared too. She left her balcony doors open every day and night, even though the chilled air bit at her, but the little cat didn't come. Seffie said Luna's disappearance had to be connected to the birds and wanted to investigate. But with Papa's trial taking place any day now, Aribella didn't want to put a foot out of line. Besides, the Doge had warned the islanders not to go out at night and there had been no news of spectre attacks. Maybe Rodolfo's reading of the stars was wrong. He hadn't been seen since his argument with Jacapo – much to Jacapo's annoyance. His gondola had gone too. The whispers around the hotel were that as Rodolfo had been threatened with seizure and checking-out, he had vanished before this could happen. Aribella and Seffie discussed it endlessly.

'We need Rodolfo here at Halfway,' Seffie had said. 'What if the stars have more messages?'

'He won't come back until he's sure Jacapo won't convince the other Elders to take his mask and check him out. And then there's all that stuff about Clara and Zio.'

'I don't know that any of it matters now.'

They went back and forth like this for hours.

The reading room was full of books of all shapes and sizes, some with furry spines, some covered in sequins, others as big as tables, and there were lots of squashy chairs to read them in. Aribella wished she could just spend the afternoon in one of those chairs looking at books instead of sorting them. The room had hundreds of shelves, some so high that they needed ladders to reach the top. It was a wonderful place for readers, but not for people who had to check overdue books.

'Wish we were dolphins,' Seffie grumbled, climbing up a ladder. 'Then we could use echoes to find the missing books in no time. I wonder if they've left Venice too?'

Any book from Rosa's list that they couldn't find on the shelves they had to check against the borrowing book. Then they had to make a note of who had taken it out and forgotten to return it. The borrowing book was leather-bound and so large that even this took ages. Its yellowing pages were covered with lists of titles, names and dates.

Today, Fin was late, and when he eventually did appear, materializing through one of the bookshelves, he caused Seffie such a shock she almost fell off the ladder. She groaned. 'Do you have to do that? You're lucky Helena's not here.'

'That's rich coming from someone who is here on punishment,' retorted Fin.

Seffie stuck out her tongue. 'At least we're not here by choice.'

'I like coming to the reading room; it's *usually* peaceful,' Fin added, as Seffie knocked several books off a shelf with a loud crash. 'Would you please be careful? Some of these books are centuries old.'

'I am being careful,' Seffie said, grabbing armfuls of fallen books. 'Ari, can you check the borrowing book for one called *The Book of Mysteries*. I can't find it anywhere.'

'*The Book of Mysteries*,' Fin muttered. He reached for the borrowing book before Aribella could and riffled through the pages. 'Oh, it's a black book.'

'What's that mean?'

'Means it contains dangerous stuff. There's only one on Rosa's list.'

Seffie scoffed. 'The only thing dangerous about a book is when it's thrown at your head.'

Fin ignored her. 'Hmm, that's strange. Someone checked it out but never returned it . . . goodness, it's *seriously* overdue! The check-out date was ten years ago. How selfish. What if someone had wanted to read it? *The Book of Mysteries* sounds quite interesting. Who took it out . . . ? Oh . . . well, that explains it.'

'What?' asked Seffie.

Fin's eyebrows rose. 'It was taken out by Zio. Makes sense that he hasn't returned it, seeing as he was murdered.'

Aribella frowned and noted Zio's name down on Rosa's list. They continued to move through the titles until Seffie finally asked, 'Why do you look so worried, Fin?'

'I'm still thinking about that book . . .'

'No surprise,' Seffie muttered.

Fin shook his head and reached for the borrowing book. 'The thing is – after Zio died, the book should have returned to the shelves of the reading room when his room was turned over for its new guest.'

'Because everyone's room is turned over when they die?' Aribella asked, remembering Seffie's tour on her first day.

'Yes, when that happens everything in the room returns to the hotel. Books should return automatically to the reading room,' Fin said. 'But this book hasn't.'

'So? Maybe the hotel forgot.' Seffie sounded bored. 'Or it disappeared when Zio's room did.'

Fin shook his head. 'Impossible. If Zio's room had been turned over, the book would be here as he was the one to check it out. But it's not, so there can't be a new guest. His room must still be his . . .'

'Does that mean he's still alive?' Aribella's skin prickled. 'That he *wasn't* murdered?'

Fin nodded slowly. 'That's what the evidence seems to suggest.'

'But where is his room then?' asked Seffie. 'Surely Rosa would have noticed there was an unoccupied room in the hotel. Unless . . . could it be the room they gave you, Ari?'

Aribella thought of her bedroom. Could it have been Zio's? She shook her head. Although Rosa had hesitated when she had handed over the key, she would have surely not given Aribella a room with such a grisly story, or it would have raised some alarm.

But there was another room unaccounted for at the Halfway, tucked out of sight . . . and maybe forgotten . . .

Aribella looked at Seffie. 'What about the locked door in the basement?'

Seffie's eyes grew wide. 'Could be . . .'

'I bet Rodolfo is right and what really happened to Zio is a clue to everything else that's happening in Venice now,' said Fin slowly. 'We have to tell the Elders.'

Aribella shook her head. 'The Elders have believed Zio was murdered for years. His portrait is a shrine with all those petals around it. We need more proof than just his room, which we don't even know for certain is his yet. If only we could get inside! And what if *The Book of Mysteries* is still there? There might be something important in it. If we could prove Rodolfo was telling the truth about Zio, then the Elders might listen to him about the blood moon too. He could come back to Halfway and continue reading the stars and make sure Venice stayed safe . . .'

'We have to get in that room,' Seffie agreed firmly. 'But how?'

'Can you walk through the door, Fin?' Aribella asked.

Fin shook his head. 'I mean, I could, but breaking in would probably set off Nymeria.'

Aribella's brain whirled. 'You always give your key in when you leave the hotel, don't you?' she said, thinking aloud.

'Yes, so?' said Seffie impatiently.

'So Zio's key must still be on the hooks behind Rosa's desk!'

Seffie's eyes widened. 'There *is* one key next to the swimming pool one, on the basement row. That must be it!'

'But how do we get past Nymeria?' Fin said. 'She'll wake up and roar in seconds if anyone tries to take a key that doesn't belong to them.'

Aribella sighed, exasperated by another hurdle. How could they get the key down from the hook and into the basement before Nymeria woke up and alerted Rosa? What they needed was to be able to move around undetected . . .

Aribella's eyes drifted to a gently ticking grandfather clock. She thought of the four clocks in Helena's training room, how the vase of flowers had reappeared across the room . . . the way the writing on the board had materialized from nowhere . . . Helena herself, suddenly moving from one end of the room to the other, all in an instant . . .

And suddenly Aribella knew exactly what Helena's power must be, and that she was the only person at Halfway who could help them.

21

'You want me to stop time so you can steal a book from one of the hotel rooms?' Helena said blankly, after Aribella, Seffie and Fin had knocked on her door, rushed into her room and told her their plan. The plan had seemed rather good in Aribella's head but now her optimism was rapidly fading. She'd forgotten how much Helena liked to follow rules. And then there had been the extremely awkward moment of explaining how Aribella had figured out that Helena's power was the ability to stop time. She decided that explaining that the room was possibly Zio's wasn't going to help their cause.

'Yes, but only so we can get information that could potentially save *everyone* from someone very evil, don't you see, Helena?' Seffie pressed.

Helena did not see at all. 'Not really,' she said. 'You don't know that *The Book of Mysteries* is going to show you anything. Sounds like an excuse to break more rules.'

Aribella gazed around Helena's bedroom in exasperation, expecting to see clocks everywhere. But to her surprise there wasn't a clock in sight. On the nightstand, Helena's cog-covered copper mask watched them. Below it, in a half-open drawer, a pincushion full of needles was visible.

'I didn't know you sewed,' Aribella said.

Helena looked surprised. 'It's just a hobby,' she replied sheepishly, but she opened the drawer and pulled out a pile of beautiful embroideries.

'These are wonderful, Helena!' Aribella said earnestly.

For the first time Aribella had seen, Helena smiled. 'Thanks, I just like it. It makes it all . . . stop. Just for a while. I hate time, hate seeing it pass, but when I sew it all melts away.' She blushed as if she'd said more than she wanted.

Aribella nodded. She knew what it was like to want to lose yourself. After all, that had been why she'd always loved going along with Theo to market. 'My papa loves to sew. He's a lacemaker from Burano.'

Helena's eyes widened. 'Really?'

Aribella nodded. 'He was. He's in prison now.'

'What?'

'There was a mix-up with the Lion's Mouth,' Aribella explained.

'That's awful.'

'It's all right. At least he's safe in prison, under the protection of the Doge. The other islanders aren't. There's something happening, Helena. Something the Elders aren't taking seriously, but Rodolfo says darkness is coming and if there's anything in the book which can get the Elders to listen, we need to find it.'

Helena's eyes flicked to her mask. 'Messing with time is dangerous, Aribella . . .'

'Please, Helena,' Aribella urged. 'Sometimes, you've got to break the rules to do something good.'

Helena looked away.

'Forget it, Ari,' Seffie said coldly. 'I knew she wouldn't help. She doesn't care.'

'I do care!' Helena protested.

'Then help us!'

Helena looked from Fin to Seffie to Aribella. Finally, she breathed out heavily. 'Fine, I'll stop time for you. But just this once and you have to just look for the book. Nothing else.'

'Thank you!' Aribella burst out.

'You're a lifesaver, Helena!' said Seffie.

'I can only give you twenty minutes,' Helena warned. 'That's the most I've ever done in training.'

'That should be plenty,' Aribella said, ignoring Seffie's frown. She knew what she was thinking – twenty minutes was not long.

Helena went to the drawer and pulled out a pocket-sized golden hourglass. 'Keep this with you. When all other clocks stop, the sand in the hourglass will start to fall,' she explained. 'As soon as the sand is gone, time is up. So long as you are holding it and Seffie's holding on to you when time stops, you'll both be able to move.'

Aribella nodded.

'When shall we do it?' Seffie asked excitedly.

They all turned to Aribella. The first flutter of nerves filled Aribella's stomach and she hesitated. What if they got caught? She was meant to be behaving . . . What if Jacapo found out and got the Doge to change his mind about freeing Papa? Would they really be checked-out of Halfway? Where would she go then? She shook these fears from her mind. It wasn't just about her and Papa. There were others in danger – the animals, the islanders and all the other vulnerable people in Venice. It was the Cannovacci's job to protect them, wasn't it? So that was what she'd do.

'No time like the present,' Aribella said, gritting her teeth. 'Let's go!'

22

'I 'll wait on the stairs,' Helena said. 'Keep checking the hourglass.'

Aribella nodded and gripped the delicate hourglass with its strange frozen sand. They crept down the staircase. The clouds had opened again and the sound of the rain hammering on the jetty echoed around the lobby. There'd be more flooding, she thought, and her resolve hardened.

But as they peered down at the lobby, Seffie groaned. 'Rosa's behind the desk!'

'I'll distract her for you,' Fin said.

They all turned and stared at him.

'Are you sure, Fin?' Aribella asked. Fin wasn't as funny as Helena about rule-breaking, but still . . . if he got caught, his reading room privileges might be revoked.

'Yes. If Helena's breaking rules, then it's the least I can do.'

'Go, Fin!' Seffie said, thumping him on the back so hard that he fell forwards.

Fin's ears turned pink.

'What are you going to do?' Aribella asked.

'You'll see. Just be ready.' Fin continued on down the stairs.

Nymeria lay in her usual place at the bottom of the staircase, doing her usual thing: sleeping.

'Morning, Rosa,' Fin said, stepping neatly over the lioness. 'This rain is something rotten, isn't it?'

Aribella and Seffie tiptoed closer.

Fin disappeared from view as he crossed the lobby.

'Yes, it really is,' Rosa said. 'I feel so bad for the poor people whose houses are flooded. It's—'

'Argh!' they heard Fin shout. 'Rosa, help me!'

'Fin! You know you're not allowed in that lounge.'

'I was just leaning on the door. I didn't mean to dissolve through . . . Now I'm stuck.'

'Stuck? How can you be stuck? Just use your power to dissolve back again.'

'It's not working – I don't know why. Can you give me a pull? Please, Jacapo will kill me if he sees me.'

'Oh, all right. If only for the sake of Jacapo's blood pressure.' Rosa sighed and moved out from behind the desk. She too disappeared from sight as she crossed the lobby.

Aribella and Seffie crept down the stairs and saw half of Fin's body sticking out of the lounge door. He winked at them as Rosa stooped to take a closer look, and began to groan. 'Ow, it hurts.'

'Really? It's never hurt you before. Come on, take my hand.'

'Now!' Aribella hissed, looking at Helena. She held on to the hourglass tightly, and took Seffie's hand.

Helena nodded and put on her mask.

A strange ringing filled Aribella's ears. Then the ringing became a rushing, and then, quite suddenly, the world went strangely quiet. The hammering of the rain stopped, as did Nymeria's snores and the usual gentle backdrop of noise from the Halfway's other guests.

It was a silence so strange that it almost felt loud.

Aribella looked up at the clock above the fireplace and then down at the hourglass. The hands of the clock weren't moving but the sand in the hourglass was. Helena had really done it. She'd stopped time.

'Amazing,' Aribella breathed.

'Thanks, now hurry!' Helena hissed.

Aribella glanced nervously at Nymeria: the lioness's eyes were half-open but she didn't stir. Seffie jumped up on to Rosa's desk and reached for the key on the basement row, next to the swimming pool key. She hesitated for a second then pulled the key off the hook.

Aribella tensed, expecting Nymeria's roars, but there was nothing but the silence.

Seffie let out a whoop and jumped off the desk. As if unable to resist, she bent down and gave Nymeria a stroke. 'Oh, she's so soft! I've always wanted to do that.'

'Stop messing around!' Helena hissed. 'You've got twenty minutes, remember?'

The sand was already falling fast through the hourglass.

Together, Aribella and Seffie hurried to the basement door and wrenched it open. Aribella winced instinctively at the screeching sound the door made, but again only the eerie silence followed. Aribella understood now why Helena found her power hard and didn't like talking about it. She hated breaking rules and must always be so afraid that others would ask her to use her power to get up to mischief. It must be so lonely for her.

They plunged into the gloom, taking the stone steps two at a time.

'This way,' Seffie called.

'Are you sure?'

'Positive.'

They plunged deeper and deeper below ground, turning this way and that. Suddenly there it was.

The locked door.

Aribella saw the key glow, just as her own key did when she was near her room. Seffie slipped it into the lock. Would it work? The mechanism seemed sticky at first, but after a bit of wiggling, the lock clicked and the door swung inwards on creaking hinges that clearly hadn't been used in years.

Seffie's hoot of triumph died in her throat as she peered into the bedroom beyond. 'What in the lagoon . . .'

The bedroom was in a state of chaos and decay. The dark purple wallpaper was stained and peeling, the rugs were moth-eaten, and every item of furniture was covered in a thick layer of dust and spiders' webs. The furniture looked as though it had been caught up in a tornado. Aribella remembered how the lobby had transformed the first time she had stepped over the threshold of the Halfway Hotel, and wondered if the same process had been interrupted here.

'It looks as though it's in the middle of a turnover,' Seffie whispered, echoing her thoughts.

'Let's get searching,' Aribella said. 'The quicker we can get out of here the better.'

She looked down at the hourglass in her hand. A third of the sand was gone.

It was dark, and neither of them wanted to touch anything so it wasn't easy. Seffie found an infestation of maggots in a drawer, which even she recoiled from. There were all sorts of strange, broken objects scattered across the floor – a smashed orb, a snapped telescope, a black box with no apparent opening – but no sign of *The Book of Mysteries*. They looked in all the obvious places – in the drawers, under the clothes strewn across the desk, in the wardrobe – and then in all the less obvious places – under and behind the furniture, inside the blackened fireplace . . . But they found no books at all.

Seffie was anxious to leave. 'Ari, we're running out of time!' she exclaimed.

Aribella looked at the sand in the hourglass, which she'd set down on the desk. There was now only a third left.

'It took us a third to get down here,' Seffie added. 'We need to go *now*.'

Aribella knew Seffie was right. But it seemed such a waste to have made it this far and go back empty-handed. The book must be here *somewhere* . . . Frantically, she scanned the room again and suddenly noticed the lumpy shape of one of the mouldy pillows on the bed. In a last desperate attempt, she raced over and slid her hand underneath, shuddering as she did. She touched the edges of something book-shaped, and felt a surge of triumph.

Could it be? Breathlessly, she pulled the book out. The cover was completely black with no markings on it all.

'Do you think this is it?' she asked, almost dancing with relief.

'It must be!' Seffie said excitedly.

'But there's no title.'

'Duh! It's called *The Book of Mysteries*, Aribella. It's not exactly going to tell you what it is. And Fin said it was a black book – that has to be it. Now, let's get out of here! This room is horrible.'

Aribella shoved the book under one arm and grabbed the hourglass. Together, they raced out of the bedroom, relieved to shut the door behind them. Seffie's hands were so sweaty as she fumbled with the key that it seemed to take for ever to turn the lock, but she managed at last.

Then they were racing back along the passageway, their footsteps pounding the stone. The book dug into Aribella's side as they twisted and turned through the tunnels until they came to the final flight of stairs.

They bounded up and tumbled through into the

warm lobby. Fin was still there, frozen in time, half his body through the lounge door. Beside him, Rosa was also like a statue, her back to them.

'I thought you weren't going to make it,' Helena called. 'Quick, the key!'

Seffie scrambled up on to the desk and put the key back on its hook. Just as she jumped back down, Aribella's ears filled with noise as everything snapped back to normal time. The world became a mess of sounds that felt louder than before – doors opening and closing on the floors above were like gunshots, the rain hammering outside like thunder. Was this how Helena always felt after setting time in motion again? No wonder she seemed so angry sometimes.

Had they got away with it? With a racing heart, Aribella looked at Nymeria, but the lioness was still fast asleep. Before Aribella could think anything else the entrance doors suddenly slammed open, and wind and rain poured in sending the candles flickering.

Aribella spun round, her mouth dropping open at the sight of the Mask Maker bursting into the lobby of the hotel. His long, matted hair hung over his distinctive beaked mask. He was drenched from head to toe and something was terribly wrong. He was stumbling, groaning and gripping his neck.

Rosa rushed to close the doors. 'Mask Maker?' she

gasped. 'Are you all right?'

The Mask Maker careered forwards, and went crashing to the floor.

'Get Marquesa!' Rosa shouted, dropping to his side.

Aribella, Seffie and Fin all rushed to the staircase but Helena had already gone. Within seconds, she reappeared with Marquesa – it was so quick that Aribella wondered if Helena had used her power once more.

Marquesa ran down the stairs. She already wore her mask – emerald-green, with rubies round the eyeholes and two painted snakes on the forehead coiled about a golden staff, the symbol of healers.

Marquesa joined Rosa at the Mask Maker's side. She pulled his cloak away from his shoulders, and Aribella instantly recognized the dark mark spreading along the man's neck. Her heart filled with dread.

Marquesa made a small sound of shock. 'I don't believe it . . .'

'What is that?' Rosa asked.

'It's a spectre bite . . . I've read about them before but I've never actually seen one.'

'So Rodolfo was right? They're really out there?' Rosa's voice trembled.

'Looks like it. And I don't have any Four Thieves Vinegar.' Marquesa cursed. 'I should have brewed some

191

more when he told me to, I should have listened . . .'

'Can you save him?'

'I'll do what I can, but I don't know. Being bitten by a creature from the world of the dead is a terrible thing. If the bite isn't treated it will spread over his entire body and once it does . . .' She stopped.

'Wh-what?' said Seffie.

Marquesa's eyes flicked to the girls. 'Once it does,' she said slowly, 'he will become the thing that bit him. He'll become a spectre.'

Marquesa pressed her hands to the mark on the Mask Maker's shoulder. Her fingers glowed with a golden light that seemed to seep into his skin. Aribella held her breath, but unlike the vinegar, Marquesa's power did nothing to help.

Aribella wished Rodolfo was here. He'd know what to do . . . She felt like everything had flipped and now she was the one frozen in time, watching everything pass by, unable to act.

Then she noticed that Nymeria was moving from her usual sleeping position. She bent her beautiful golden head to the ground, coughed and from her mouth tumbled a balled piece of paper that rolled right up to Rosa's feet.

Rosa picked it up and unfolded it. Her face paled and her hands started to shake.

'What does it say?' asked Marquesa, her eyes still fixed on the Mask Maker.

Rosa's hands shook so badly that the paper almost ripped in two.

'Rodolfo,' she whispered. 'It says Rodolfo is responsible for this.'

23

Bruno was called to carry the Mask Maker up to Marquesa's suite. It was odd to see the man who had frightened Aribella so much in the shop thrown over a boy's shoulder as if he were nothing more than a rag doll.

Marquesa hurried up the stairs after them, muttering about herbs she'd need. 'Maybe I can brew a batch in time. I don't see how it's possible . . . but I must try.'

Rosa followed. 'Whatever I can do to help, let me know.'

Without a word, Aribella, Seffie, Fin and Helena hurried to Aribella's room, only daring to speak once they'd filed in and closed the door. Then their voices tumbled over each other's, with Aribella quickly filling in the background so Helena was up to speed. Helena listened calmly and Aribella was glad she was with them.

'Was the Mask Maker really attacked by a spectre?' Fin said.

'And why did Nymeria cough up Rodolfo's name?' asked Seffie.

'I'd have thought if anyone was safe it would be the Mask Maker,' Helena said.

'Did the mark look the same as the one on your friend, Ari?' Seffie whispered.

Aribella nodded. 'Exactly the same. It was definitely a spectre that bit him.'

Helena shook her head. 'Oh, this is bad, very bad. Did you see how shocked the Elders looked? Rosa was shaking . . . And I can't believe Rodolfo is the one behind everything. I mean, why would he try to warn everyone about the spectres if he was making it all happen?'

'To look clever, perhaps?' Fin suggested. 'Or maybe to make himself appear innocent?'

'I'm sure that's how Jacapo will see it,' Seffie muttered darkly. 'It's a bit of a coincidence that Rodolfo was there that night the spectre attacked your friend. But I still find it hard to believe he's evil.'

'Me too,' Aribella agreed passionately. 'He saved me and Theo, remember.' She didn't believe it, couldn't believe it.

'Still, it does look suspicious that he's disappeared . . .' said Fin.

'Maybe he's been kidnapped by the real person behind all this,' Seffie protested.

'Yes. Or maybe he's in hiding because they know he's on to them,' Aribella added. 'Maybe that person put Rodolfo's name in Lion's Mouth to cover their own tracks.'

'Do you mean Zio?' asked Helena.

'He can't be dead. We were just in his room. And the book he borrowed was there too.' Aribella held up the black volume. *The Book of Mysteries*.

'It's got to mean he's alive, right, Fin?' Seffie said.

Fin turned as pink as he always did when Seffie talked to him directly. 'The fact this book didn't return to the library after Zio was meant to have died, I would say that yes, he is likely still be alive.'

Helena's eyes widened. 'That's why you wanted it? To prove Zio wasn't murdered?'

They all nodded.

'You didn't tell me that part,' she said sourly, crossing her arms. Aribella could tell she felt left out.

'I'm sorry we kept so much from you, Helena,' Aribella said. 'But the Elders have been ignoring what is happening. Thanks to you, we have a chance of finding out the truth before it's too late.'

Aribella placed the plain black book on her bed. Seffie and Fin huddled round to look. Helena uncrossed her arms and joined them.

Seffie sniffed. 'I know they say you should never judge a book by its cover but . . .'

Aribella opened the book carefully, expecting the pages to have decayed like everything else in Zio's room. But they were pure white and pristine, as if the book was brand-new. There were three hundred pages of dense text, and no contents page or index.

Aribella leafed through the pages, feeling a wave of hopelessness. 'We need someone to read this, and fast. Do you think Julietta's speed applies to reading?'

'Doubt it,' said Seffie. 'Maybe Helena could freeze time in twenty-minute stints.'

'Ugh, that would be exhausting,' said Helena. 'Breaking the rules once was one thing. But I would have to do it . . . about a hundred times to read all this.'

Fin cracked his knuckles and rolled his neck. 'Don't worry,' he said smugly. 'I'll get through it faster than anyone else at Halfway, no Cannovacci power needed.'

'*Reading is the greatest power there is,*' Aribella murmured, repeating Rosa's words. 'Thank you, Fin.'

Fin nodded, already riffling through the delicate pages with practised ease. 'Well, seeing as Helena actually broke hotel rules, and the world as we know it is in peril, I think pretending to get stuck in a door and reading a book is the least I can do.'

Helena hid her face behind her hands. 'Don't remind me!' she groaned.

'It's a shame dissolving through walls isn't more useful,' Fin joked, keeping his eyes on the page, but Aribella could tell this bothered him.

'It *is* a useful power, Fin,' she said. 'You need to believe that. The Mask Maker said true power comes when we let go of false masks and accept ourselves as we truly are,' she added.

Fin looked up long enough to give her a small smile before returning to the book.

Aribella tried to smile back but found she couldn't. She kept thinking of how frail the Mask Maker had looked hanging over Bruno's shoulder, of the hideous black mark on his neck. He had seemed so powerful. If a spectre could attack him, what hope did anyone else have?

Helena was clearly thinking the same. 'I can't believe the Mask Maker was attacked,' she repeated, as if trying to get her head round it.

'Did you see Nymeria do anything?' asked Seffie suddenly. 'I mean, before she coughed up Rodolfo's name.'

Aribella shook her head. 'No, why?'

'Exactly!' Seffie exclaimed. 'She didn't do anything. She just kept sleeping, even when the Mask Maker came in injured. There's something wrong with her at the moment and that's bad news. I'm going to find out what, but in the meantime it seems we can't rely on Nymeria to tell us when Venice is in danger – or even the Mask Maker.'

'I hope he doesn't die,' Helena said. 'He hasn't had an apprentice for years. And then what will the Canno-vacci do? What will Venice do?'

Aribella tried to comfort her. 'There's still hope if Marquesa can make the antidote in time.'

But even she knew this was a slim hope. Marquesa had said the Four Thieves Vinegar took twelve hours to brew. The mark would have spread by then. She recalled how swiftly even a few drops had worked on Theo's wound that night on the lagoon with Rodolfo . . .

And that's when it came back to her – the vial Rodolfo had given her. What had she done with it? She had put it in her pocket.

Aribella's heart skipped a beat and she rushed over to the wardrobe, threw open the doors and rummaged around in the back of it for her old clothes, wishing desperately for the vial to have survived Rosa's laundering.

'Aribella, now is not the time for an outfit change,' Seffie called.

Aribella ignored her. It had to still be here . . . it had to be! She found her old clothes. They felt more scratchy and rough than ever. Had she really worn these every day only a few weeks ago? It already felt like another life.

She plunged her fingers in the pockets of her trousers, feeling for the vial. Aha! It was still here – thank the lagoon, it was still here! She pulled the vial out, her heart racing.

There was still a little of the gold liquid left inside.

There was no time to explain. Aribella raced up to the fourth floor. She did not know which suite was Marquesa's, but the sweet scent of brewing herbs drew her to one of the doors, which was ajar.

Clutching the vial tightly to her chest, Aribella knocked and pushed the door open. 'Marquesa?' she called.

The entrance room was full of soft cushions and low tables with softly glowing lamps and pretty patterned tablecloths. A potion was bubbling in a brass pot over the fire. Was that the Four Thieves Vinegar? It was green and seemed a long way off turning gold.

'Marquesa?' she called again, louder this time.

There was a groan from a door to her right. Aribella rushed over to it.

The Mask Maker was lying on a low couch, his eyes closed, his cloak and mask removed. His aged body looked oddly shrunken and child-like. The beaked mask was propped on a stand on a side table, watching with its empty gaze. The Mask Maker's face was kinder and more vulnerable-looking than she'd expected. He looked ordinary, like someone's grandpa. For the first time, Aribella wondered about the Mask Maker's family.

He gave a moan, turning his head, and with a sharp intake of breath she saw the mark from the spectre bite again. It was already darker and had spread down his neck and across his chest, reaching, with webbed veins of black, towards his heart.

Hurrying, Aribella moved closer. She fumbled with the vial, but before she could unstopper it, the Mask Maker's eyes snapped open.

He reached out and grabbed her wrist.

'Clara?' he groaned, his eyes rolling back in his head. 'Clara?'

Aribella's skin went cold. She looked behind her, half expecting to see someone there. But they were alone in the room. He must have been hallucinating. It must have been an effect of the spectre bite, or whatever relief Marquesa had given him in the meantime.

'Forgive me, Clara,' the Mask Maker wheezed, gripping more tightly. 'You must forgive me. I shouldn't have made it, I was tricked.'

Made what? The Mask Maker sounded as if he was talking in riddles.

He turned towards her, staring wildly. 'I was a blind fool. I didn't see that it would break the boundary.'

Break the boundary?

'But you did, didn't you, Clara? That's why you took it. You were always so clever . . .' The Mask Maker trailed off, his eyes rolling back into his head.

Aribella couldn't yet make sense of what the Mask Maker was saying, but it felt extremely important. She tried to focus on the vial. She needed to pour some drops on to the bite. But where did she start? His neck? His chest? There were only a few drops of the remedy left: what if she wasted it in the wrong place? There was no room for mistake.

'Stay with me, Signore,' she said. 'Stay still.'

But he was tossing and turning. 'Clever girl. I am sorry . . . I broke the oath of the Mask Maker when I made it. Keep it safe, wherever it is . . . or else the world is doomed.'

'Keep what safe?'

'He used my weakness against me. He flattered me

. . . Zio . . .'

Aribella's skin tingled. Zio *was* at the heart of this. And Clara too.

She remembered how proud the Mask Maker had been showing her his collection. *The best in Venice.* That's what he'd said. Zio must have asked the Mask Maker to make him a mask, and Clara had taken it.

She tried to stay calm. 'Signore, please keep still. I'm trying to help you.'

But his arms and legs were thrashing wildly. It was hard to open the vial with the Mask Maker still gripping her. She finally got the lid off and reached towards him. But his other hand shot out to grab her, knocking the vial out of her grasp. It fell on to the floor where the golden liquid spilt and was absorbed instantly into the rug.

'No!' Aribella cried. She dropped to her knees next to the vial, but it was all gone.

'Forgive me, Clara?' the Mask Maker asked, his eyes wide. 'Please. The darkness . . . I feel it coming. I am sorry for what I did. I should have told the truth long ago . . . I knew he would come for his revenge.' He put a hand over his heart. 'Give me this final wish.'

Aribella swallowed. She didn't even understand what he wanted to be forgiven for. And anyway, it was Clara's forgiveness he sought, not hers . . .

The Mask Maker's eyes were full of anguish so she nodded, hoping it would be enough. She saw the flicker of an expression pass over his face – something like acceptance or peace – then he closed his eyes, and lay back, finally still. He was dead. Aribella knew it at once. She felt sick and numb. She'd never seen anyone die before. Her whole body began to shake as she stared at the Mask Maker's lifeless corpse, at the horrid black mark covering his chest. For a moment, it felt as if Helena had stopped time again, and she was the only thing still moving. And then the door opened behind her. She turned.

'Aribella? What are you . . . ?' Marquesa's eyes moved to the Mask Maker. She dropped the fresh herbs she was carrying.

'He's dead,' Aribella whispered, her shoulders shaking uncontrollably. 'He's dead.'

24

arquesa made Aribella move to the fire. She gave her a cup of sweet hot cocoa and wrapped a thick blanket around her shoulders. Rosa was there too, her face pale. Aribella knew there were things she needed to tell the Elders – *important* things – but she was too shell-shocked to speak.

'We shouldn't have left him,' Marquesa muttered.

'It wouldn't have made any difference,' replied Rosa, and after a moment's pause, 'How bad are these spectres, Marquesa?'

'Bad, if the old stories are to be believed.'

Rosa shivered. 'I didn't really believe they were a threat until tonight. I feel a fool.'

Marquesa shook her head and said softly, 'None of us did. It's very hard to believe nightmares until you see proof.'

'I don't understand what's wrong with Nymeria either,' Rosa went on. 'Why didn't she wake when the Mask Maker came in, or before? She should have. I'm worried she's sick. Venice could be in great peril and we'd have no warning.'

'It is strange,' Marquesa agreed, frowning.

'Are you feeling any better, Aribella?' Rosa said, turning to her.

'I'll give you some potion to help you sleep,' Marquesa said, and disappeared into another room.

Rosa took Aribella's empty cocoa cup from her. 'I'm so sorry, Aribella. We should have been here. We thought it would be quicker to gather ingredients together.'

'I had some Four Thieves Vinegar. I could have saved him.' Hot tears spilt from Aribella's eyes.

'Hush,' Rosa soothed. 'It wasn't your fault.'

Marquesa reappeared, holding a round glass container full of pink liquid. She was looking confused.

'What is it?' Rosa asked.

'My sleeping potion . . . I had a large amount of it in my stores. Enough to knock out an army, but this is all that's left. It's not hard to brew but I wonder who took it? And why?'

Rosa's eyes widened. 'You don't think someone has

been drugging Nymeria, do you?'

Marquesa looked serious. 'Rodolfo is the only one who has disappeared . . .'

Rosa shook her hand. 'I can't believe that of him.'

'We didn't believe it of Clara, either,' Marquesa muttered.

For a moment Aribella wondered whether to mention Zio and everything that she and her friends had discovered, but her thoughts were so scrambled. She didn't know what to think or where to begin.

Rosa took her arm. 'Come on, you've been through enough already tonight. Let's get you to bed.'

Rosa escorted Aribella up to her room and made sure she drank every last drop of the potion.

'I need to tell you something,' Aribella murmured as she slipped between the sheets.

'Shush,' said the key keeper firmly. 'We'll talk in the morning.'

The potion sent Aribella into a sound and dreamless sleep that lasted the whole night. But when she woke the next morning the Mask Maker's lifeless body reappeared in her mind's eye so that even the bright sunshine streaming through her window could not take away the coldness she felt. She lay in bed, staring at the canopy above her, trying desperately to make sense of it all.

The Mask Maker was dead. He had been killed by a spectre. He was a Cannovacci, a Mask Maker, and he'd been killed because he had made a forbidden mask. For Zio.

Zio and Clara . . . Clara and Zio . . . the two names went round and round in her head . . .

A part of her wanted to hide away from it all in bed, but she knew that was no good. Now, more than ever, *someone* had to find out what was happening, and right now Aribella, Seffie, Fin and Helena might be the only people who could do that. Where *was* Rodolfo? A part of her felt angry with him. Even if he was about to be checked-out, she couldn't help feeling that he'd abandoned them. And now he was suspected of killing the Mask Maker and drugging Nymeria! But he had said that she had to trust him, and she would – she didn't believe he had done such awful things. But the accusation meant he wouldn't return any time soon. It was up to them.

So despite everything, she got up, dressed and hurried down to breakfast. The weather had not improved since last night, and wind and rain lashed at the windows.

The dining room was practically empty. Hardly any Elders were there. They were probably having a council meeting. She agreed with Rodolfo: the Elders seemed to spend far too much time discussing things and too little time acting. Ursula sat alone. She looked paler than ever, and she was dressed for winter, in a white fur coat and white gloves. As their eyes met, she smiled and came over.

'I'm so sorry for what you went through last night, Aribella,' she said softly. 'We all see now that Rodolfo was telling the truth.'

'Why didn't you see it before?' Aribella asked. 'Couldn't you see it in his thoughts?'

'Rodolfo's thoughts have always been hard for me to read. He's good at hiding things.'

'But why didn't you see the truth in my thoughts, then? I saw the spectre with my own eyes.'

Ursula grimaced. 'Forgive me. It was a mistake. And I should never have told Jacapo about your visit to the Doge. I think it's fortunate you told the Doge to warn the Inbellis. I'm sure Jacapo will agree after today's meeting, especially now the spectre's existence has been proven beyond doubt. Have you had any news about your papa's trial, by the way?' she added earnestly.

Aribella shook her head and felt a stab of shame as she realized she hadn't thought about Papa once today.

Ursula gave her a sympathetic look. 'I've heard the

Doge's sickness has worsened so maybe it's been delayed. But try not to worry. Do you have any other family on Burano island? Other friends, perhaps?'

Aribella looked away. Did she? Did Theo still think of her as his friend? She felt another stab of guilt. He probably still believed she was locked up in the Doge's palace with Papa.

Aribella wondered if Ursula read this in her thoughts, because she said, 'Well, by way of an apology, if you ever want to visit anyone on Burano, my gondola is yours to take whenever you need.' With a gloved hand, she reached into her pocket and pulled out a wooden miniature of her own gondola, which she handed to Aribella. Just like Rodolfo's, the *permesso* was an exact replica, perfect in every detail, right down to the pink cushions.

Aribella stared at it in surprise. It was the last thing she'd expected from Ursula. 'What about Jacapo? He said I wasn't to go out again.'

Ursula pressed the miniature gondola into Aribella's hands. 'I will deal with him. It's the least I can do after I got you in trouble for doing the right thing. Please use it whenever you need. But perhaps not tonight – there's a full moon, and I worry what that might mean. We don't know when the next blood moon will come, now that Rodolfo has gone.'

Aribella thanked her and took the *permesso* to the table in the corner where Seffie, Helena and Fin were sitting.

'What happened last night?' Seffie asked, looking worried. 'You just ran off. And Rosa said the Mask Maker died and that you were there . . .'

Helena looked worried too, and Fin didn't look like he'd slept at all. When he tried to butter his napkin instead of his toast and Seffie pointed this out, he just muttered something about being up late reading.

Though she didn't want to relive the events of last night, Aribella told them what had happened, as well as everything the Mask Maker had said to her before he died.

When she'd finished the other three stared at her in stunned silence. For the first time ever, none of them had touched their plates of pastries, not even Seffie.

'What do you think that means?' Fin asked. 'So Zio forced the Mask Maker to make a mask for him and Clara hid it? Does that mean she wasn't really bad or that she was? Or was the Mask Maker bad? Oh, my head hurts trying to understand all this.'

'And where are Zio and Clara now?' Seffie asked. 'I mean, if he's not dead, maybe she isn't either? Maybe she's hiding too. She could come and tell everyone the truth.'

'That's what I'm wondering,' Aribella admitted. 'Among a million other things.' It felt as if there was a dark cloud hovering over Venice, an unstoppable storm.

'And what kind of mask can break boundaries?' Helena added thoughtfully.

'The boundary . . . Of course!' Fin sat up abruptly. 'Helena, you're brilliant! Everyone, meet me in the reading room in ten minutes,' he blurted, shooting up from the table so fast that they all jumped.

'What? Why?' Seffie groaned. 'I've had enough of that place to last a lifetime.'

'Just do it,' Fin whispered fiercely, and he raced out of the dining room.

25

Ten minutes later, Aribella, Seffie, Fin and Helena were all in the reading room, huddled round a table in the furthest corner, out of sight of the door. Fin took *The Book of Mysteries* from the shelf where he had hidden it, and showed them a page excitedly. Most of it was taken up with a drawing of a beautiful mask with the golden face of a lion.

'Whose mask is that?' asked Seffie.

'It's not anyone's. It's the Mask of Venice. I just finished reading this section last night . . . Listen.' Fin read out: ' "*The legendary Mask of Venice is a mask so powerful it would allow the owner to pass freely between the worlds of the living and the dead, thereby bestowing immortality upon them. However, were its full power to be wielded on the Island of the Dead during a blood moon, it could result in the boundary's complete destruction . . ."'*

Fin stopped. 'This is what I think the Mask Maker made. What Clara took and hid.'

The four of them exchanged terrified looks. If a Mask like that existed, then it wasn't just Venice in danger but the whole world.

It was Seffie who spoke next. 'Stupid fool, why did he make a mask like that?'

'Seffie! You shouldn't speak ill of the dead!' Helena exclaimed.

'He said he was tricked,' Aribella said.

They all exchanged looks again.

'We could be getting the wrong end of the stick, you know,' Fin said. 'Maybe the Elders are right and it really is Rodolfo and this Clara person who are causing the spectre attacks . . .'

Aribella shook her head. 'Why would the Mask Maker want forgiveness from Clara if that was true? And he didn't mention Rodolfo at all. It must be Zio who killed him. Maybe because he doesn't know where Clara hid the Mask of Venice. Maybe he's even trying to get Rodolfo out of the way by putting his name in the Lion's Mouth. We're the only ones who know the truth. We have to find Zio.'

'But how?' asked Helena. 'We don't even know where he is.'

Helena was right. Where in Venice could Zio be hiding?

'Well, hopefully we'll be safe for a bit,' said Seffie, flopping back in her chair. 'Surely there won't be another blood moon for a while. It was ten years between the last two.'

They reflected on this and fell silent. How long would it be until the next blood moon exactly? Aribella wondered. If only Rodolfo had been more precise. Aribella thought back to the last blood moon and remembered the mist – and the strange island that had seemed to rise out of it.

'Fin, is there anything else in that book about the Island of the Dead?' she asked.

Fin shook his head. 'It only says that it appears on blood moons. Its exact location is unknown.'

'I think I saw it,' Aribella said. 'That night of the last blood moon, with Theo.'

Seffie shivered.

'So the boundary is already weakened?' Helena asked.

'Maybe because the mask is on the island,' Aribella said.

'Could be,' Fin said slowly.

'And there's a full moon tonight,' Aribella went on.

They looked at each other fearfully.

'If that's true, we have to find it before Zio does,' Seffie exclaimed.

'And we have a *permesso*, thanks to Ursula.' A plan was coming together in Aribella's mind.

'Rowing on to the lagoon at night with spectres on the loose doesn't seem very safe,' Fin said sceptically.

'I don't care, it's a chance to find the mask,' Aribella said. 'And the spectre was frightened by fire. If it appears again I could try to fight it off.'

'Well, I'm coming with you,' said Seffie.

Aribella knew her friend well enough by now to know that there was no use protesting.

'All right,' she said, feeling relieved.

'Are you sure you should go?' Fin asked. 'It's so risky.'

'Life is risky, Fin!' Seffie replied. 'In case you've forgotten, some madman who's supposed to be dead might open a secret boundary and let in a whole bunch more of those evil spectres.'

'Fair point,' Fin relented. He sighed and looked at Helena. 'We'll help too.'

Helena nodded. 'Whatever you need.'

That evening, Aribella did not undress. Instead, she lay on her bed fully clothed, listening, with growing trepidation, to the wind and rain lashing against her windows. It would not be an easy row in these conditions. She'd felt numb all day, but now her body surged with adrenaline.

She remembered lying on her bed at Papa's house, also fully dressed, that first night she'd met Rodolfo. So much had happened since. And it had all led to this.

At quarter to midnight, she got up and pulled on a thick wool cloak and leather boots. She pocketed Ursula's *permesso* and collected her mask from the nightstand. She put it on hesitantly, half anticipating a sharp sting. But no sting came. The mask seemed to be behaving. She tied the ribbons, hoping that nothing would go awry while they were on the lagoon.

She watched the clock until midnight, then stepped out into the corridor.

Seffie and Fin were already there, waiting. Seffie, like Aribella, was cloaked and masked, but Fin was still in his nightclothes, his feet bare. He gave Aribella a swift nod.

'Ready?' Aribella whispered.

Fin nodded again. She could tell he was nervous. 'You?' he asked.

'Ready as I'll ever be.'

'And Nymeria is definitely with Marquesa?'

Aribella nodded. The healer had had Nymeria brought up to her room so she could keep an eye on her while the sleeping potion wore off.

'Good luck, Fin,' Seffie whispered.

'And to you two,' he whispered back. 'Come back in one piece.'

'And you try to stay in *two* pieces for as long as you can,' Seffie replied.

Fin gave her a small smile then stepped halfway through his door. Half of his body dissolved into the room beyond. 'Rosa won't believe this for long after last time,' he warned, 'so you'd better be quick. I'll count to twenty and then start shouting.'

'Thanks, Fin,' Aribella said, before she and Seffie hurried away down the staircase.

They made it to the first floor where they hid around a corner and waited.

After a few more seconds, they heard Fin's voice yell down from above. 'Rosa! Help! I'm stuck.'

'Fin?' Rosa's voice called back from somewhere below. 'Is that you?'

'I was sleepwalking again, Rosa. I'm stuck in my door . . .'

'Not again!' Rosa groaned. 'I thought you were strong enough to get out of this by now.'

'I thought so too. But I need my mask. Please . . . If Jacapo finds me, he'll kill me . . .'

'This is the last time, Fin. I swear. I'm going to start

tying you to your bed.' They heard Rosa's footsteps coming up the staircase. 'This sleepwalking has to stop!' she muttered to herself as her footsteps travelled to the floor above.

Well done, Fin, Aribella thought. She and Seffie did not hesitate a moment longer. They raced down to the lobby, treading as lightly as they could. They crossed the lobby floor in a few large strides, pulled open the entrance doors and slipped out into the stormy night.

The wind howled in their ears as they shut the doors. Aribella's heart was hammering. A small flutter of triumph rushed through her but she quashed it. They might have got out of Halfway, but that was only the beginning.

They hurried along the jetty, shivering in the cold rain. The sky was dark and neither the stars nor the moon were visible through the dense layer of cloud above them. The wind sent Aribella's hair lashing around her face and both their cloaks flapping. It seemed to have picked up even more since night had fallen, and if it was this bad here on the sheltered canal, Aribella didn't want to think about the conditions on the exposed lagoon.

She gripped Ursula's *permesso* tightly and pulled on the mooring rope, humming. Ursula's gondola came rushing up to the surface. At the prow was a lantern, miraculously already lit. This time, Aribella was glad of the gondola's covered carriage; at least it meant Seffie would be dry.

'You go in and shelter,' she whispered as they clambered aboard.

But Seffie was having none of it. 'If you're going to be out in the wet then so am I.'

Aribella sighed. 'Sometimes you are too stubborn for your own good, Seffie.'

'I'll take that as a compliment,' Seffie retorted, untying the rope.

Aribella took up the oar, pushed the gondola away from the jetty and started to row. As before, she soon got into a rhythm and the gondola felt easy to propel, as if it weighed nothing. There was no one around so they were able to move quickly, though the pummelling rain greatly reduced visibility and the Grand Canal was so overflowing with glistening, black water that it was hard to tell where its banks ended. The mask protected her face against the wind, and she willed the gondola onwards.

The rain worsened as they emerged on to the lagoon. Aribella gritted her teeth as the rain seeped through her cloak and down the back of her neck. She wished there were stars visible to light the way but she could manage without them, for she knew the route back to Burano by heart. She rowed out towards the open lagoon, getting into even more of a flow, so that soon, the gondola was skimming over great stretches of black water as if it was nothing. The speed took Aribella's breath away.

When they got near enough to see the outline of Burano ahead of them, Aribella halted the gondola.

Ahead of them was a light on the water. A fishing boat. 'Seffie, look!' she said. But as Rodolfo had once told her, her mask made her unwatchable but not unhearable.

'Who goes there?' said a familiar voice at once.

Aribella's mouth fell open. 'Theo?' she stammered.

26

ribella and Seffie quickly pulled off their masks as
Theo held up his lantern, illuminating his face.
His fringe flopped into his eyes and he pushed it
back and gazed at her, his expression a mixture of
shock, wonder and confusion.

'Ari? Is that you?'

'Theo, what are you doing out here? You shouldn't
be fishing at night. Didn't you get the Doge's warning?'

'What warning?' Theo's forehead creased. He was
looking at her as if she were a ghost.

The Doge was meant to have told the islanders not
to go on the lagoon at night. Had he been too sick to do
so? And come to think of it, where were the guards
he'd said would be patrolling? Now it occurred to her,
she realized they'd seen none as they passed the palace.

'I asked him to warn you——'

'You asked *the Doge* to warn me?' Theo scoffed.

'Well, to warn all the islanders. There's something . . . evil out here.' How could she get Theo to understand? He'd never believe her if she started talking about spectres. Theo had no time for anything he thought was nonsense, and it was clear he remembered nothing about being bitten by one of them himself or else he would not be here in the dark, fishing alone. Whose boat was he using anyway?

Theo shook his head. 'Where have you been all this time? I thought you were . . . And who's your friend?' He eyed Seffie distrustfully and his gaze travelled over the gondola. 'And *where* did you get a gondola?'

Aribella cursed inwardly, hating how this must look to him. 'I-I can't really explain, Theo . . . but you don't have to worry, I'm fine . . .'

'Yes, I can see that,' Theo said with a coldness that did not suit him. 'Didn't think to let me know sooner?'

'Theo . . .' Aribella felt desperate. How could she explain? She'd signed an oath to keep the secret of the Cannovacci.

'I've been trying to get an audience with the Doge ever since you disappeared,' Theo continued. 'I've been worried sick about what might have happened to you, I thought you and your papa were in prison.'

'Papa *is* in prison,' Aribella said quickly, clutching at the one truth she could tell.

'What?' For a second, Theo's face softened, but then his expression hardened again. 'Why should I believe you? Turns out Gian was right about you this whole time; you don't care about me, you never have.'

'Please, Theo. That's not true. Of course I care about you.'

'Then where were you? After I almost drowned in the storm that night I expected you to visit but you didn't. Then I found out you were missing and I was afraid. I thought something awful had happened. I *blamed* Gian for putting your name in that stupid Lion's Mouth. But I shouldn't have wasted my time. Here you are swanning about in a gondola. You just left me behind without a backwards glance.'

He was jealous, of course he was. That was why he was so angry. To him it seemed as though she'd got the very thing he'd always dreamt of, and had decided not to share. He thought she'd forgotten him, and he was hurt. Aribella felt awful. The last thing she'd ever want to do was cause Theo pain.

Tears sprung to her eyes. 'Theo, it's not like that. I promise.'

'Then what *is* it like, Ari? Tell me.' Underneath his anger Aribella could see he still held a tiny glimmer of hope that he was wrong and that there really was another explanation. That she hadn't just abandoned him.

She shook her head. 'I wish I could explain, Theo, but I can't.'

The hope left Theo's eyes. 'Gian's a better friend than you are. I should have listened to him all along. He lends me his boat now that mine is gone. He won't come out at night because he still believes those silly ghost stories like the rest of them – but at least he hasn't abandoned me.'

His words stung, but there were bigger things to worry about right now. It was good that the other fishermen weren't coming on to the lagoon. Theo needed to stay away too.

'You shouldn't be here, Theo.'

Theo scoffed. 'Why? Because of you? Are you a witch, Aribella? Going to curse me?'

Seffie had been watching silently. 'Ari really can't explain!' she interrupted. 'You wouldn't understand.'

Aribella wished Seffie hadn't said anything.

'I wouldn't understand?' Theo said, his voice rising. 'I'm just a stupid idiot, like Gian, like the rest of the islanders – is that right?'

'No, Theo, of course not,' Aribella gasped.

'I defended you.' His voice was thick now. 'I saw the

flames at the market that day and you know what I thought? I thought that no matter what she's my friend, and I'll stick by her because she's good and kind. But a good, kind friend wouldn't just disappear without a word.'

Aribella couldn't bear it. She ached to tell him the truth. To tell him everything.

'Theo, I–!' She screamed suddenly as the mask in her hand gave a hot sting.

Not now. Not here.

'Ari?' Seffie called.

Aribella threw the mask down on to the carpeted floor of the gondola, cradling her hand.

'Did it sting you again?' Seffie asked. 'Like in the palace?'

Aribella nodded. 'It was worse, like . . .' She stopped. The colour of the water around the boat had changed. It was no longer inky black . . . She looked up to the sky and a cold hook of dread took hold of her. A patch had cleared in the clouds, and through it the full moon was now visible. A moon that was not white and pale as it ought to be, but red.

Blood red.

'Seffie, the blood moon!' she cried out.

THWACK. Something hard and solid collided with the back of Aribella's head. She stumbled forwards, her ears ringing, trying to keep her balance. She heard Theo shout and Seffie cry out her name. Aribella looked round to see a cloaked, hooded figure standing right behind her in another gondola, wielding an oar. For a moment, everything seemed to move in slow motion. Rodolfo, was Aribella's first confused thought. But it didn't look like his gondola. And he wouldn't attack her. So who was it? And why?

Her mind raced, reaching for explanations, but then the oar hit with her head again and she was knocked sideways out of the gondola. She heard Seffie screaming and Theo shout her name as the world flipped upside down, and Aribella plunged, head first, into the icy water.

27

Aribella kicked upwards desperately but her cloak was dragging her down . . . Her lungs squeezed . . . she was running out of air . . . Suddenly, arms clasped around her waist and Aribella was propelled upwards. She broke the surface and gasped. Her chest was tight and her throat burned with salt. She coughed painfully and the arms around her loosened.

'Ari, are you all right?' Seffie shouted over the wind. 'Hold on, I'm going to swim us to the gondola.'

Seffie put her head down and started kicking hard, still gripping Aribella. Aribella tried to kick too, but her legs were only getting in the way. Her cloak was hindering their progress. She unleashed the clasp and let it sink. Without it, they moved more easily and soon made it to Ursula's gondola. It was overturned, and they clung to the side.

The wind roared in Aribella's ears. The waves seemed enormous. Above, the blood moon shone down, and fresh fear filled Aribella's heart as she saw that Theo's boat was nowhere to be seen. She had to hope he had rowed to safety. She tried not to think that he might have abandoned her, as she had abandoned him.

The cloaked attacker had disappeared – and, she realized with a lurch, so had her mask. It had been in the bottom of the gondola.

'Oh Seffie, I've lost my mask!' She felt sick with shame and tears rolled down her cheeks. 'I've ruined everything. It's all my fault.'

Seffie shook out her wet curls and frowned. 'Ari, none of this is your fault. And the boundary isn't open *yet*. There's still time to find the island. But not if we stay here crying.' Seffie's green eyes flashed fiercely. She was being so strong and brave that it made Aribella feel stronger and braver too. 'Let's get this gondola the right way up. The *permesso* will help us.'

The *permesso*! Aribella felt another wave of despair. For the miniature gondola was in the pocket of her cloak, now at the bottom of the lagoon along with her mask. She tried to stay positive, but without a working gondola what hope did they have of getting to the Island of the Dead and stopping Zio?

'It was in my cloak,' she told Seffie. 'It's lost too!'

'Hold on,' said Seffie. 'I won't be long.' She put on her mask and dived down into the dark water.

'Seffie!' Aribella gripped the side of the gondola and peered into the water's murky depths. A few bubbles popped up. But for several minutes, Seffie did not reappear. Aribella felt horribly afraid that something had happened to her friend. But just as she was starting to panic, Seffie's head resurfaced.

'I found something even better,' she called.

Beside her, the noses of two large dolphins broke the water. They tipped their heads back and made clicking sounds. Aribella stared at the beautiful creatures in amazement.

'I knew they hadn't left, Ari. And they knew Venice would need them . . . Clever things. They'll be able to take us right to the island. They can find anything.'

'That's great, Seffie!' But during the time Seffie had been underwater, Aribella had decided what they needed to do. 'Now you have to get one of them to take you back to the Halfway Hotel. I'll go on to the island alone.'

'What? No way!' Seffie protested, just as Aribella had known she would.

'You have to go back to Halfway and tell Rosa,' Aribella replied firmly. 'Now we know it's a blood moon and there's an attacker out on the lagoon, we need as much help as we can get.'

'Come back with me,' Seffie said. 'We can get help together.'

Aribella shook her head and looked up at the crimson moon. 'I don't think there's time. I will try and find the Mask of Venice before Zio can. Besides, spectres are afraid of fire so I should be able to hold them off for a while.' But without her mask, for how long . . .

'I don't want to leave you.'

'You have to.'

For a moment, Aribella thought Seffie would continue to protest. But she could see Seffie knew this was their only chance.

'All right. But if you die on that island, Ari . . . I-I'll kill you,' Seffie said fiercely.

In spite of everything, Aribella laughed. 'Go now. Quickly. The sooner you can get help the better.'

Seffie nodded. 'I'm not saying goodbye. I'm saying see you soon,' she said firmly.

Aribella nodded, unable to reply, hoping that Seffie was right.

Seffie reached out and held on to one of the dolphin's fins, before making clicking noises at the back of her throat.

'I've told this one where to take you,' she said. 'Just hold on to its fin when you're ready.'

The first dolphin turned in the direction of the main island and started to move away, taking Seffie with it.

For a moment, Aribella watched as Seffie and the dolphin sped back towards the main island. Her friend Seffie, who was a living, breathing reminder that there was good in the world, good that was worth fighting for. She turned back to the lagoon. On the horizon a thin line of white separated sea from sky. The mist.

Pushing her fear down inside her, Aribella gently took hold of the dolphin's fin. The skin felt smooth and slippery but she managed to get a grip. The dolphin gave a powerful kick of its tail and propelled them through the water. Spray rushed past them as they cut through the waves.

All too soon they were inside the mist and it engulfed everything so that Aribella could see nothing but hazy whiteness around them. She gripped the dolphin's fin more tightly, scared she'd slip off and be left behind. The dolphin kept speeding onwards. Then, the mist cleared and everything was bathed in that terrifying red light from the blood moon again. And in the middle of the water was an island.

The Island of the Dead.

It looked just the same as before – floating strangely in the mist, just as deserted and frightening. This time, with the dolphin's help, she got close enough to see wind-blasted trees and vine-choked cherubim above the door of the crumbling palazzo on top of the central hill. As they neared the shore, the dolphin slowed. It seemed afraid to move any closer, and Aribella didn't blame it. She let go of its fin.

'I'll swim the rest of the way,' she said, hoping it would understand. 'Thank you.'

She looked into the dolphin's eyes and somehow knew that it did. How could people ever think animals didn't have thoughts and feelings the same way people did? Seffie was right, you only had to look a creature in the eye to know.

With aching limbs and a heavy heart, Aribella dragged herself through the last stretch of choppy water towards the island, trying not to think about what might confront her. She wished she had her mask. She was doing this for Theo, she reminded herself, and for Papa and Seffie, and for everyone else in Venice.

As soon as she reached the shore, the rain stopped and the wind dropped. An unsettling silence pressed against her ears. Aribella shivered as she hauled her exhausted body up from the water and stood on the beach. The sand looked as if it were made of fragmented bone.

A gondola she didn't recognize was beached on the

shore. She'd never seen a gondola out of water before and there was something unnatural about the way it was lying there on its side, like a wounded animal. She searched the hull for the winged lion, but could see only the remnants of a symbol. This had to be the gondola she'd seen on the lagoon. Her cloaked attacker was already here.

Nervously, Aribella looked up towards the ruined palazzo on the hill. A light glowed in the window of the top turret. A fresh prickle of fear crawled down her spine.

Was Zio up there? Did he already have the Mask of Venice?

There was nowhere else to go but towards the light.

She had no plan, no mask, and no one to help her. Her power was barely under her control and she had no idea if she'd be able to use it without her mask. It was suddenly hideously apparent how powerless she really was against this great evil that threatened Venice, this Zio who had thwarted the other Elders. She was just a thirteen-year-old girl . . .

But if the Halfway had taught Aribella anything, it was that sometimes the impossible *is* possible.

She had to try.

nother cloud scudded across the blood moon, throwing bands of light and shadow ahead. How long would the blood moon last? Aribella wondered as she climbed the hill. What would happen if she was on the Island of the Dead when it disappeared? Would she disappear too?

All her instincts screamed to turn back, but she concentrated on putting one foot in front of the other. Her breathing grew heavier with every step. Her mouth was dry. It felt so odd, this silent, slow progress towards certain danger, like the terrifying calm that often falls before the worst storm.

The frigid air pressed Aribella's sodden clothes to her tired body. She continued on, growing colder and colder. Her fingers prickled in anticipation. But could she control her power without her mask?

It wasn't far now. The ancient walls of the palazzo gleamed in the red moonlight. Clumps of rotten ivy clung to the crumbling walls. Gargoyles lined the roof, blackened with soot, missing faces and wings. The stone cherubim over the entranceway were so choked in vines that it looked as if their mouths were open in silent screams.

The wooden door was half rotten, but when Aribella pushed it the hinges did not screech. Goosepimples rippled across her skin. She hesitated, peering into the gloom beyond. For a moment, she thought she could not bring herself to move a step further, but she forced herself on.

The courtyard inside was in a severe state of disrepair. There was a stench of stagnant water and the ground was littered with rubble. Many of the surrounding pillars were missing so that it looked as if the floors above could come crashing down at any moment. The stone staircase looked as if it was disintegrating.

Aribella held her breath. The air was pulsing.

A shadow moved across the edge of her vision. Aribella whirled round, her heart pounding, imagining a spectre. But the shadow was gone. Was her mind playing tricks? Her nerves were already so frayed, the last thing she needed was imagined fears on top of all her real ones.

Aribella picked her way across the courtyard, treading as quietly as possible across the rubble. But as she moved, she saw something that made her blood run cold.

A body lay on the ground. Her heart lurched. His floppy hair was unmistakeable.

Theo.

Aribella scrambled over the rubble towards him. Theo was unconscious, his skin ice-cold, but he was breathing. She whispered his name but he did not respond. She dropped to her knees, checking his face and neck, and gasped. For on his neck was the black bite of a spectre. And this time there was no Four Thieves Vinegar or Rodolfo to save him.

'Aribella?' called a soft voice behind her. It was a voice that Aribella recognized but for one disorientating moment could not place ... Then she realized who it was. Relief washed over her as she whirled round and saw the figure at the foot of the staircase. They were saved. Seffie had managed to get to the Halfway in time.

'Ursula! Oh, thank goodness. I'm so glad you're here. You have to help. Theo has been bitten.'

'How did you get here?' Ursula's voice was sharp.

'Is anyone else with you?'

At this, Aribella's relief faded and confusion replaced it. Then the pieces of the puzzle began to slide into place.

'It was you,' she said slowly, her voice breaking. 'You're the one who's been helping Zio. You've been on his side the whole time. You drugged Nymeria!'

How had she not seen? How had none of the Elders seen? But Ursula could read other people's minds which means she could manipulate them. Aribella had mistaken her for someone who fainted and cared too much about her appearance. She'd mistaken her for being kind.

Aribella felt a nudging in her head. She tried to protect her thoughts but it was no good.

'So it's just you. Good.' Ursula seemed to relax.

'Why would you help him?' Aribella cried.

'Because he's going to give me what I want.'

'And what's that?' Aribella spat.

'What everyone wants: to be young and strong and beautiful for ever. When Zio is master of both worlds he can give me this. Do not judge me,' she added. 'You're young. You do not know yet what it's like to age, to see your beauty and power fade.'

'There are more important things,' Aribella replied passionately. 'Like kindness and goodness, honesty, bravery, friendship.'

For a moment, Aribella sensed Ursula falter, but then came a cold laugh above them.

'Friendship?' said another voice that Aribella, once again, recognized but could not immediately place.

She looked around the shadowy loggia for the speaker.

'Friendship makes you weak, just like all the other Cannovacci. But tonight, that changes. For too long, I have been forced to waste a potential that is my birthright. But after tonight I will no longer be subject to the rules of those who are beneath me.'

The speaker appeared at the top of the staircase. For a moment, Aribella was so stunned that she did not believe it. For there in white robes, his face covered as usual by the glittering diamond mask, stood the Doge of Venice.

29

'You're Zio?' she whispered, shock coursing through her. This couldn't be right. It didn't make any sense. The Doge was kind and good and sick. The fishermen had always loved him. He'd cared for the poor islanders for decades. He'd promised to help Papa . . .

The Doge lifted his gloved hands and removed the diamond mask. Aribella recoiled. Underneath was a face she'd seen half of before – in Zio's masked portrait at the Halfway Hotel, with the white petals laid underneath. The pale skin of the portrait now looked half-dead – grey and blistered – exposing bone beneath. His teeth were black. And his pale blue eyes fixed upon her.

'But how?' she stammered. 'It's not possible . . . You

were a guest at the Halfway . . .'

Zio's lips turned up in a sneer. The effect of this on the rest of his rotten face was ghastly. 'Ten years ago, when Clara stole the Mask of Venice from the bonding room – stole *my* mask – she made me believe she'd hidden it here, on the Island of the Dead. Clara meant to trap me, you see. And it almost worked for I did not find it before the blood moon began to fade and the island disappeared. I escaped but I paid a price . . . My soul split from my body that night. As I had bonded with the Mask of Venice, so my soul was able to occupy the body of Venice's leader – the Doge. All this time I have waited for the next blood moon and my next chance.'

'You k-killed the Doge?' Aribella stammered, horrified.

'Not yet. But soon, when I am done with him, he will part of my spectre army. As you will be. And your little friend.'

'Never!'

Zio smiled. 'For a moment I thought *you* were Clara, brought back to life . . . Did you think so too, Ursula?'

Ursula did not respond. Aribella couldn't look at her. How could she have helped Zio for the sake of her own vanity? Now everyone at the Halfway, everyone in Venice, was going to die.

'Where is Clara?' she asked.

Zio's smile became a scowl. 'Perhaps she is also between worlds, half-alive, half-dead, too weak to claim a body. No matter. Everyone assumed she murdered me, thanks to a little help from Ursula.'

'You made people think Clara was a murderer when she was trying to protect Venice!' Aribella gasped.

'Honesty, bravery, friendship,' Zio sneered. 'What does any of that matter? All that matters is power.' He reached into his robe and held up another mask.

She knew it immediately. The scratched, unremarkable-looking face. *Her mask.* Aribella stared.

And all of a sudden a memory came rushing back to her.

She was in the Mask Maker's shop. She could see the black curtain swaying ahead, only it seemed a lot bigger. Or she was a lot smaller. There was a woman there – a woman with long dark hair.

'Shh, Aribella. I just need to look for something. Stay here.'

Aribella stayed on the floor, but there was light underneath the curtain, changing from blue to green to orange. She crept towards the curtain and crawled under it, gazing up at the stand in the middle of the room – just as she had when she had visited the Mask Maker's for her fitting. Only this time the stand wasn't empty.

A beautiful golden mask was fastened to it, a mask with the face of a lion.

Aribella gazed up at it and the face seemed to turn to her, seemed to see her. And she felt the same feeling she'd had looking in the Mask Maker's mirror, a feeling of belonging, of coming home.

'Aribella, get out of there!'

Aribella snapped back to the present with a jolt. Her head was ringing and her heart was beating impossibly fast. Finally she knew the truth. Her ugly old mask was the Mask of Venice. It had chosen her in the shop because – somehow – she had bonded with it as a child.

And Ursula had drawn her out on to the lagoon, had told her of the full moon, had given her a *permesso* to make it easy . . .

Her fingers tingled. Could she use her flames to kill Zio? She'd only have one chance. And if the real Doge was still alive in that body then she might harm him too . . .

'I have waited so long for this moment,' Zio said. 'I thought the last blood moon would be my only chance. But as the boundary has been weakened so another blood moon came, much sooner this time. I knew you were connected when you came to the palace – though you lied. Ursula told me about your mask afterwards.

But I felt it. I felt its power, calling to me.'

So that explained the stinging Aribella had felt at the palace and just now on the lagoon . . . The mask must have felt Zio close both those times. She shivered. *Maybe it's trying to get back to him.* Was that what it had been trying to do this whole time? Had her name already been scratched out in the lining and replaced by his? Was the mask Zio's now? Or was it still deciding its true owner? If she could show the mask she was worthy of its power, would it choose her again, as it had in the shop?

'I took my revenge on the Mask Maker too.' Zio laughed cruelly, and Aribella's insides clenched in horror. 'I will not wait in hiding any longer. Tonight, with the Mask of Venice, I will break the boundary for good and raise my spectre army.'

Zio lifted the mask to his face and tied the black velvet ribbons behind his head. As soon as he raised his face up to the red moon, the mask began to change. Its surface turned golden. The scratches smoothed and a mane formed round its edges. The nose expanded and its mouth stretched. A headdress of tiny jewelled rubies appeared across its forehead. It had become the head of a lion, just like the drawing in *The Book of Mysteries*.

And there was no longer any mistaking. This was the Mask of Venice.

'Come, my army of the dead!' Zio raised his hands and a ghastly hissing filled the air. All around the shadowy edges of the courtyard, white skulls began to appear. Aribella moved closer to Theo and bit her tongue to stop herself screaming.

The spectres gleamed under the red moon. Hundreds of them.

30

Fear ripped through Aribella's body. Even if she managed to summon her fire power now, there was no way she'd ever be able to fight this many spectres without a mask. Even the strongest Elder wouldn't be able to stop them single-handedly.

'My spectres!' Zio's voice was strong now. 'You've waited patiently for me to fulfil my promise. And tonight, I will. Tonight, I tear down the boundary between death and life so that you may exist in the realm of the living for ever with me as your ruler!'

The spectres hissed their applause.

'And y-your promise to me, Zio?' Aribella had almost forgotten about Ursula. She had pressed herself against the crumbling walls, and looked terribly afraid.

'My promise to you?' said Zio coldly.

'Y-you p-promised that I would never grow old.'

'Ah, yes. Well, you shall have your wish. You will never grow a second older than you are at this very moment. Spectres!'

The spectres rushed forwards, surrounding Ursula.

Ursula cried out in fear. 'No. You can't! I helped you!'

'You did,' Zio replied in that same cold, thin voice. 'But you are no longer useful to me.'

'No!' Ursula screamed in horror as the spectres swooped down upon her.

For a moment, Aribella could see nothing but skulls, and hear nothing but hissing and screaming. She watched, paralysed with fear. When the spectres dispersed a few moments later, there was nothing left of Ursula except a new skull, rising from the place where she had been, indistinguishable from any of the others and certainly not beautiful as Ursula had always wanted to be.

Aribella stood in front of Theo.

'Sweet,' Zio scoffed. 'But he's already been bitten. He will soon be a spectre too and part of my glorious army. What an honour for a lowly Inbellis fishing boy.'

Aribella looked up in despair. Her breath caught. Already the moon was paler in colour, more orange than blood-red. She struggled to remember how long it had lasted the night she'd seen it with Theo. *An hour – two?* If Clara's original plan had been to trap him on the island until the blood moon passed, maybe Aribella could do the same. If she could keep Zio talking then the blood moon would pass before Zio could unleash his army of spectres on the living world, and the Island of the Dead would disappear with him on it. With her and Theo on it too . . . She swallowed. But Clara had made a sacrifice that night long ago, and Aribella must too. It was too late to save Theo and herself, but maybe she could still save Venice.

'Why did you kill Ursula?' she stalled desperately. 'Don't you care about anyone but yourself?'

'Caring is weak.'

'That's not true,' Aribella replied fiercely. 'My friends make me stronger.'

Zio laughed. The sound was horribly high-pitched. 'You are too soft. Soft and *weak.*'

Aribella tried to think of another question when, once again, a shadow crossed the edge of her vision. This time she was certain her mind wasn't playing tricks. It wasn't a spectre. Who else was here? Aribella looked around the upper levels of the courtyard but couldn't make out anything between the dark archways of the loggia.

Aribella's stomach clenched. Was this it? The end?

She looked back at Theo. She'd failed him. She'd failed the world. If it wasn't for her, Zio would never have got the mask back. She should have kept it safe in her room in the Halfway. How could she have been so stupid? For a moment, she felt hopeless but then she pulled herself together. No, none of this was her fault. It was Zio's. And if this was really the end then she wasn't going to let it happen without a fight.

She drew herself up to her full height, and looked Zio defiantly in the eye. Summoning her strength, she felt her power stir. Aribella focused on the vibrations, letting them pass through her body. Heat built up inside her. Her fingers tingled and she raised them in front of her.

'Spectres!' Zio called.

Aribella tried to quell her fear and concentrated on herself, her power. As the spectres swooped on Aribella, flames shot from each of her ten fingers. Flames stronger and more powerful than any she'd made so far. The spectres fell back, hissing. Aribella would not be able to hold them off for long. The pain was excruciating without a mask.

Through her agony she heard Zio laughing. Was all hope lost? The flames in her hands started to dip . . .

But beyond Zio, on the loggia, something *was* moving between the columns. And this time, Aribella could see that it wasn't a shadow. It was something solid, small and furry, with a long tail . . .

'Luna!' Aribella breathed in amazement, just as the cat sprang on to the back of Zio's head and clawed wildly at the mask's ribbons. Zio roared and whirled to face his unseen attacker. But Luna had already torn right through the ribbons. So as Zio turned, both Luna and the Mask of Venice flew into the air, the cat landing neatly on her paws at the top of staircase and the Mask of Venice bouncing down towards Aribella . . .

Zio howled in fury but Luna leapt past him, bounding after the mask. She grabbed it in her mouth and raced towards Aribella, dodging the spectres and ducking under Aribella's flames. She dropped the mask, face down, by Aribella's feet. Aribella could see Zio's name in the mask's lining, but there too, still faintly visible, was her own name, and she knew at once what Luna meant her to do.

She let the flames die, then grabbed the mask and shoved it on to her face. She managed to tie the broken ribbons just as the spectres pressed forwards once more.

The mask immediately began to sting but she gritted her teeth. *No*, she told the mask. *You chose me. You belong to me too.*

A warm feeling began to stir inside her, replacing

her fatigue. Power soared through her body, stronger than ever before. Her hands were shaking and she clenched them into fists, feeling her power build. The mask stopped stinging.

'You're wrong,' Aribella shouted as the spectres swooped towards her. 'Caring about others doesn't make you weak, it makes you strong.'

She opened her hands and enormous licks of fire shot out. The spectres wheeled away, screaming.

'How is it you can use *my* mask?' Zio cried. He closed his eyes and pressed his fingers to his temples.

Aribella's flames flickered as she felt the mask resist and begin to sting once more. Her eyes watered with pain. Zio was calling it, and the mask was wavering. The spectres pressed in again. She summoned her power, concentrating hard.

You belong to me, she told the mask. She would not let the Mask of Venice belong to Zio. She would not let him use it to kill innocent people and rule the world with terror. The mask still wavered. The stinging worsened. Aribella could barely concentrate on anything other than the pain. She felt so alone and small and helpless. Another surge of pain made her cry out and stumbled. The mask's broken ribbons came loose and it slipped from her face.

No . . .

Her flames shrank back into her fingers. The spectres rushed in. This was it. The end . . .

Aribella heard a fierce roar above her. She looked up dazedly and saw that, silhouetted against the blood moon, was an incredibly sight: a lioness with beautiful golden wings outstretched.

Nymeria!

And on Nymeria's back, one looking slightly queasy and the other very determined, were Fin and Seffie.

Aribella wasn't alone. She had friends who loved her and were prepared to put themselves in harm's way to save her. And as she held on to this truth, she reached down for the Mask of Venice and put it back on her face, tying the ribbons again defiantly.

She thought with all her might: *You are mine.*

31

The *crack* that resonated inside her skull as the mask broke in half was like the sound of the earth splitting in two. Ringing filled Aribella's ears as the ribbons came apart again, and the two pieces of the mask fell to the floor with a crash that echoed around the courtyard. The pieces landed in the rubble and dust, lifeless and plain once more.

The spectres instantly disappeared with howls of collective fury.

'No!' Zio cried, falling to his knees.

The features of his face began to melt away from the skin, like a waxwork in a flame, and with a final grimace, were replaced by the kindly ones of the old Doge. He slumped to the ground.

Aribella heard cheering above and looked up to see

Seffie and Fin beaming down at her.

'You did it, Ari!' Seffie whooped. 'You actually did it! You defeated Zio.'

But they weren't safe yet. Aribella looked up to the dark sky. The blood moon was no longer red or orange, but turning white. Zio was defeated but they were still going to get trapped on this godforsaken island. Nymeria could not carry them all at once.

Mist had moved in and the beach below had already gone. She heard the sound of crashing water as a wave rushed through the courtyard door. The walls of the palazzo were beginning to crumble. As soon as the bricks and mortar came tumbling down they turned into dust and were whipped away by the wind.

Aribella scrambled for Theo and tried to support him. He was too heavy. 'Luna,' she called desperately. The island had fallen away on all sides and water surrounded them. The floor of the courtyard cleaved in two. They were marooned on a few shrinking patches of land.

'Get to the beach!' Fin called, gesturing frantically.

And there, slicing through the mist, with a glowing lantern at its prow, was the curved *ferro* of a gondola. At the stern, his cloak billowing and his star-covered mask flashing, was Rodolfo.

Her heart leapt for joy.

'Jump in,' he called, speeding towards her. 'Quickly!'

Aribella did not need to be told twice. Rodolfo helped her lift Theo into the gondola and then pulled Aribella in too. No sooner were they both aboard than the piece of land they'd been standing on sank below the water with a final whoosh.

'The Doge!' Aribella gasped.

But Rodolfo was already rowing towards the patch of ground where the Doge's body lay. He was so frail and light that they pulled him into the gondola easily. His eyes were closed but, like Theo, he was still breathing. Aribella looked around desperately for Luna. She had saved them, they couldn't just leave her . . .

Aribella's heart stopped. At the top of the crumbling staircase stood a woman in a mask, holding Luna. She was shoeless and her dress was dirty and torn. Her long, dark hair fell across her face and she wore a mask covered with flowers, birds and silver fish. When she removed it her eyes were shining with so much pride that it made Aribella's heart ache. She knew who this was, though she'd not seen her for ten years and barely remembered her from before that.

But she knew.

Mama.

Aribella struggled to breathe. After everything that

had happened tonight, this was the biggest shock of all.

Rodolfo smiled as he reached out to grab the woman's hand and pull her aboard. 'So the stars were right. Welcome back, Clara, I've been waiting for you.'

'Hello Rodolfo. And hello Aribella, my darling girl,' replied Clara.

Luna meowed, and she sounded a different cat entirely. Aribella looked from her mama to Luna. 'It was you all along,' she whispered.

Suddenly she swayed with exhaustion and found she couldn't support herself any longer. Clara caught her. Her arms were warm and soft. And though her clothes were dirty, her skin smelt of sweet jasmine, and the scent took Aribella back to memories she'd forgotten – evenings in a garden, with Papa laughing, deep and bellowing, and Mama singing the folk songs of the gondoliers . . .

Rodolfo sang now as his gondola flew across the dark water, leaving the disappearing Island of the Dead far behind. Aribella let the melody wash over her. She saw Nymeria, Fin and Seffie flying ahead, leading the way – Fin holding tightly to Seffie. They left the mist behind and in the clear night sky beyond the moon was silver again, as it should be, and the stars twinkled brightly.

In her ear, Mama whispered, 'You've done so well,

my darling. You've been so brave. Stronger than I ever could have imagined.'

Aribella felt as if her heart would burst. She was too tired to reply but pressed herself closer to her mama, afraid she would disappear again. She thought back over all the times Luna had been there. Every time she'd hurt herself, or been teased by Gian, or cried because of Papa's silence . . . Luna had been there, with her warm body and soft fur, to cuddle and comfort her. If only Aribella had known that it had been Mama, trapped in the cat's body as Zio had been trapped in the Doge's! If only she'd known that – this whole time – she'd never truly been alone, as she'd thought, but was being watched over by someone who cared for her.

'Theo's been bitten . . .' she murmured.

'Don't worry about him,' Rodolfo called. 'Io tells me Marquesa's latest batch of Four Thieves Vinegar is ready. He'll be fine. And thanks to you, so is Venice.'

'Sleep now,' Mama whispered. 'We'll soon be home.'
Home.

Aribella closed her eyes but held on tightly. She didn't think she'd ever let go again.

32

A ribella woke to the delicious smell of hot cocoa and the feel of silk sheets against her skin. She tried to stretch, but her body protested. Her limbs ached as if she'd recently swam the entire lagoon.

Slowly, Aribella blinked her eyes open. She was back in her bedroom at the Halfway.

Seffie, Fin and Helena were perched on the end of her bed, playing cards, and Rodolfo, Rosa and Marquesa were seated in armchairs by the fireplace, drinking from china teacups. Io was hanging off the arm of Rodolfo's chair, and, blocking the doorway, was Nymeria, wide awake for a change and making the large bedroom feel suddenly small. Aribella remembered Nymeria flying last night and looked for her wings, but there was nothing to be seen. Had that really happened? Had any of it? Her aching body told her it had. Mama sat in a chair closest to her bed, wrapped in Rodolfo's star cloak and with Luna asleep on her lap. She looked down into Aribella's eyes and her smile was so full of happiness that, for a moment, Aribella forgot all her aches and pains.

She couldn't believe it. Clara was her mama, and she was actually *here*. At the Halfway. *Alive.*

She glanced at the empty mask stand beside her bed and was surprised to feel a twinge of loss. It had been an evil mask, *Zio's mask,* she reminded herself. But it had also been partly hers, and it had helped her defeat Zio in the end. Now she had no mask at all. Could she still be a Cannovacci? She pushed the thought from her mind; for now she was just happy to see everyone safe and alive.

At the end of her bed, Seffie squealed, 'Aribella's awake!'

There was a flurry of limbs, then Aribella's view was blocked completely by her friends as they tumbled on top of her.

'Let her breathe,' Rodolfo called. 'Imagine, Aribella survives Zio and his spectre army on the Island of the Dead only to be suffocated by you three in her own bed.' He chuckled.

Seffie, Fin and Helena fell back reluctantly. They sat

up on their knees, wearing matching grins. Aribella tried to smile back but it was painful to move her face.

'You'll ache, I'm afraid,' Marquesa said kindly. 'That was a lot of power you used without a mask.'

The cuckoo made everyone jump as it shot out of the clock.

'Almost lunchtime! We've been worried about you,' Seffie said. 'You were out for hours.'

'How's Theo? And the Doge? Are they all right?' Aribella asked, struggling to sit up.

'They're both fine,' Marquesa assured her, crossing the room to plump Aribella's pillows. 'Luckily, I had the batch of Four Thieves Vinegar I'd brewed for the Mask Maker. I wasn't sure how effective the potion would be on your friend Theo a second time. But it seems to have worked just fine. Not one but *two* spectre attacks . . .' She shook her head. 'I'm not sure anyone in history has ever been so unlucky.'

'Or *lucky*, given the boy survived both times,' Rodolfo interjected, his eyes twinkling. Aribella smiled at him, it was so good to see Rodolfo back at the Halfway, where he belonged.

'Yes, I suppose that's one way to look at it,' said Marquesa, laughing. 'Anyway, he has been restored to full health and is back on Burano with his family. We even manged to recover his fishing boat, which

Nymeria discovered floating away over the horizon. We've returned that safely too.'

Aribella was so happy to hear Theo was all right. And even that Gian's boat had been recovered.

'Drink some cocoa,' Marquesa instructed. 'It will make you feel a good deal better.' Rosa raised her palm and a china cup full of steaming cocoa appeared in Aribella's hands. Marquesa wouldn't let Aribella say another word until she had drunk several large gulps. The cocoa was warm, sweet and restoring. Aribella instantly felt better.

'And the Doge?' she asked.

'Resting,' Marquesa replied. 'Back at the palace. Ten years of harbouring the soul of Zio has taken its toll, but after examining him I am satisfied that he will recover well in the care of his own physicians.'

'He ordered the immediate release of your papa, Ari,' Seffie added, 'and arranged for him to be taken home to Burano, cleared of all charges.'

Aribella's heart leapt as the burden of guilt and anxiety about her papa finally lifted. Clara gave her hand a squeeze and Aribella looked up at her, unable to find the right words. She leant back against her freshly plumped pillows and struggled to put the remaining pieces of the puzzle together. 'What about Zio?'

'Gone,' Rodolfo assured her.

'At last,' Clara added. 'Ten years ago, when I tried to trap him on the Island of the Dead, I should have known that his soul would escape.'

'And you ended up as Luna?'

Clara nodded. 'We both escaped the Island at the last moment, but our souls split in the process. I wanted to stay close to you, Bella, until the Mask of Venice was brought to the island again, and I could return to normal.'

'And cats do have nine lives!' exclaimed Seffie. 'So you knew you wouldn't be hurting her or anyone. Not like Zio used the Doge.'

Clara smiled and looked down at the cat in her lap fondly. 'She was the perfect host. But she'll need a new home now.'

Seffie's eyes popped. 'Oh, can I have her as my companion, Rosa? Please?'

Rodolfo and Rosa exchanged glances. 'Novices aren't allowed pets, as you know,' Rosa said. 'But I think we can make an exception this time.'

Seffie looked as if she was about to explode with happiness.

'Could Zio do it again?' Aribella asked nervously.

Rodolfo shook his head. 'No. The Mask of Venice broke last night, thanks to Aribella's strength and refusal to give in. It was destroyed. Zio is gone.'

'For good?' asked Seffie.

'For good,' Rodolfo replied firmly.

'Yay!' Seffie exclaimed, giving Fin a high five and clapping Aribella on the back. 'Well done, Ari!'

Aribella smiled, despite the pain it caused her. She was so relieved. 'What happened to you after you left me, Seffie? How did you get Nymeria to fly?' she asked, remembering the incredible sight of the golden lioness soaring over the Island of the Dead, with Seffie and Fin riding on her back.

'When the dolphin took me back to the Halfway, the Elders were already in the lobby,' Seffie explained. 'They already knew something was wrong because Nymeria had recovered from Ursula's sleeping potions and was up on her feet roaring. As soon as she saw me, she growled and said, "Climb on." So while the other Elders were getting their gondolas, me and Fin climbed on to Nymeria's back. Her fur is so soft, Ari, you wouldn't believe it! Then she ran outside to the jetty and took off into the sky! It was amazing, Ari!' Seffie's eyes shone with pride. 'We flew so fast. But I was still so worried we wouldn't get there in time, until I saw Rodolfo's gondola in the mist and I realized she wanted to lead him to you.'

Rodolfo nodded. 'It was very hard to know the way

in the mist. But Nymeria was my guide.'

'I'm so glad we made it,' Seffie added, her voice thick. 'Helena helped with that bit.'

Everyone turned to Helena, who shrugged sheepishly. 'Just a little,' she said, smiling.

'Thanks, Helena,' Aribella said.

'No problem. From what I hear, you were doing a pretty good job on your own.'

'Did you see all this in the stars?' Aribella asked Rodolfo.

Rodolfo nodded. 'I'm sure you must have thought I had abandoned Venice, but I assure you, I never did. For many months, I'd seen hints in my star readings of what was to come, but it was only a few weeks ago that I finally understood. The stars are curious guides. Everything is possible until the moment it happens, if that makes any sense, and often if one variable changes a completely different set of events are set in motion . . . Are you following this?'

'Yes,' Fin and Helena said at once.

Aribella and Seffie exchanged looks.

'Kind of,' Aribella said slowly. 'So you're saying that if one thing didn't go how you'd seen it happen in the stars then the rest of the sequence would cease to come true too.'

'Exactly. There are normally many ways to reach

the same end. However, in this case, I was dismayed to see that while there were hundreds of possible sequences where the boundary was destroyed, there was only *one* way for events to unfold where the mask would be destroyed and the boundary could be saved. And that was down to you, Aribella. I had to let things unfold in the only way they could to save Venice. You had to be there alone. If I had been there, I would have helped – or tried to. So I had to keep silent and hope that you would trust yourself and your power.'

So Rodolfo had known what was going to happen. He'd let her go to the Island of the Dead, let her face Zio alone. Aribella wondered if she should feel angry but, if the events of last night were the only way to defeat Zio and destroy the Mask of Venice for good, then she would do it again, a thousand times over. And Rodolfo had come to help in the end, she reminded herself, at the moment she needed it most.

'As soon as I discovered the truth, I knew that Ursula must not find out that I knew. In case she told Zio that you were capable of destroying the mask,' Rodolfo continued. 'If he'd known he would have killed you as soon as you stepped foot on the Island of the Dead, maybe even before. And once Jacapo threatened to take my mask I knew I had to leave the Halfway. I hid on an island on the lagoon, watching the stars, waiting for my time to help. I knew that, when the next blood moon came, I would need to be there in the final moments, but that if I intervened before then, Venice was doomed.'

Aribella nodded but Seffie didn't seem satisfied. 'Couldn't you have told us *anything?*' she huffed. 'A little warning would have been nice!'

'Ursula would have read anything he told us in our thoughts,' Fin said.

'But Aribella almost died!'

'I do understand your indignation, Persephone. I must ask you to forgive me – and you, Aribella – for the danger I put you in. But I knew it was the only way to save other lives. And I knew that you were strong enough to fight Zio. Do you know why you could still use the Mask of Venice even when its true owner, Zio, was there?'

'Because I bonded with it when I was little,' Aribella replied.

Rodolfo shook his head. 'That's why you could *use* it. But it chose you because your power was stronger that Zio's.'

'No it wasn't!' Aribella protested. 'He had a whole army of spectres.'

'You were stronger because your power came from love for your friends. Zio was driven by fear: fear of being forgotten, of becoming powerless.'

Aribella nodded, thinking she understood. She reached for Clara's hand. 'Did you know Clara was my mama? Is that why you came for me alone that first night, without telling the other Elders?'

Rodolfo nodded slowly. 'I suspected. Remember, all the Elders believed Clara to be a murderer. I was not sure how they'd take to her daughter. I wanted to see what you knew first in case I needed to warn you to keep quiet, or worry about Ursula hearing anything in your thoughts. But you knew nothing about her so I deemed it safe to bring you here.'

Aribella suddenly felt exhausted trying to connect everything in her head. She was sure it would all make sense later but for now there was too much to understand.

'Well, that is a lot of information to take in on an empty stomach,' said Rosa. 'I propose a breakfast feast. What does everyone say?'

'But it's lunchtime,' said Helena.

'So what?' said Rosa, and Helena smiled.

'So what,' she agreed.

Seffie and Fin cheered.

'Thank goodness!' exclaimed Fin. 'I'm starving. Riding a flying lioness really gives you an appetite!'

Twenty minutes later, they were all in the dining room, tucking into the best breakfast the Halfway Hotel had ever seen. There were stacks of all Aribella's favourite pastries, plus cream cakes with cherries, chocolate éclairs and two types of pancakes drizzled with lemon and sugar or chocolate and strawberries. At Rosa's insistence, Clara was sent to have a bath and change into a clean dress. Her face was shining when she entered the dining room in a pale blue gown and she looked more beautiful than ever.

'Ten years of eating fish scraps,' she groaned. 'I've missed the Halfway's pastries.'

'I still can't believe you were Luna,' Seffie marvelled. 'No wonder I couldn't understand you. I was worried my power was failing or something!'

'Yes, I must have perplexed you. The thing is, I had no idea how to speak cat!'

'It's not that hard,' Seffie teased.

Clara laughed. 'Is that right? I wish we could have swapped places!'

'Me too!' Seffie smiled. She and Clara seemed to like each other already.

Outside the hotel windows, the sky lightened, fading from indigo to cyan, and as the sun rose it painted the windows gold.

Seffie shot to her feet. 'Listen! Can you hear that?' she exclaimed, running to the windows and flinging open the balcony doors.

Everyone fell silent and listened. It started with a few tweets, then a few dozen, and soon a cacophony of birdsong billowed into the room. It was such a beautiful, bright and happy sound. Aribella's heart lifted. The birds had returned!

Everyone crammed on to the balcony to watch as hundreds of birds of all shapes, sizes and colours swooped over the Grand Canal. Aribella hadn't even known such an amazing variety existed in Venice.

But it wasn't just the birds that made them all cry out with delight. The water of the Grand Canal was back safely between its banks, and all the parts of the city that had previously been submerged – the narrow, winding *calli* and open, paved *campi* – were safely above water again.

Seffie was tweeting away. 'My friends are back for good!' she reported gleefully. 'Now the danger has passed and the city is safe again.' She hugged Aribella and Fin and Helena. Fin went bright pink and Helena looked pleased.

Clara pulled Aribella into her arms too. And the words that Aribella had been waiting to say finally came out as tears spilt down her face.

'I missed you so much, Mama.'

'I missed you too, my Bella. But I was always there watching over you.' Clara pulled her closer and stroked her hair. Aribella felt so safe and warm that she could have stayed in her mama's arms for ever. 'Shall we go and see Papa and your friend Theo?'

'Oh yes!' Aribella said, then hesitated. 'But what will you tell Papa?'

Clara smiled. 'I'll think of something. I imagine it's going to be quite a shock for him.'

'It will be, but he'll be so happy. I'm so happy,' Aribella replied firmly.

'Me too.'

Jacapo appeared on the balcony. He regarded Clara fearfully. Aribella had to remind herself that Jacapo had thought Clara was a murderer for many years. It was going to take many of the Elders a little time to get used to the idea that she wasn't. Aribella supposed she couldn't judge Jacapo too harshly, given she'd briefly considered the idea that he had been the one helping Zio.

'It appears some apologies are in order,' he said stiffly. 'To both of you,' he added, his eyes flicking towards Rodolfo.

But both Rodolfo and Clara waved his apologies away.

'You were trying to protect Venice,' Rodolfo insisted, which Aribella thought was very good of him.

Jacapo nodded. 'Rest assured, Zio's portrait has been removed from the building. Clara's, which I've learnt you kept without permission, Rodolfo –' he stopped, as he struggled to hold himself back from telling Rodolfo off for this – 'will be put back in its rightful place on the Halfway's walls.' Jacapo turned to Aribella. 'Thank you, Aribella. For your service to Venice.'

'Perhaps a reward is in order?' Rodolfo suggested.

Jacapo's lips pursed. 'The Cannovacci do not protect the city for reward, Rodolfo, as you well know.'

'But a small one might be nice. Given the pain Aribella's family has been caused.'

Jacapo looked as if he wanted to protest, but instead

he sighed. 'What do you suggest?'

'Anything you'd like, Aribella?' said Rodolfo, his eyes twinkling.

Aribella was about to shake her head when a thought occurred to her. 'Signore, if it is all right, I do have one idea . . .'

Soon, their pockets stuffed with pastries, Aribella and Clara were gliding along the Grand Canal, each steering a gondola.

Clara had Rodolfo's *permesso* to use his gondola, and Aribella was steering Ursula's old gondola, which had also been found on the lagoon by Nymeria, floating close to where Aribella and Seffie had left it. The gondola was unrecognizable as hers. The pink cushions and cabin had changed to plain wooden benches.

'Rodolfo, really,' Jacapo had spluttered when Aribella had stated her requested reward. 'Do you really think that's wise?'

But in the end, he'd relented, and even provided the new *permesso*.

As they reached the mouth of the Grand Canal, the bells of Venice began to toll. At first there were just a few, and then others joined in, so that it felt as if the whole city was singing.

'What are the bells for?' Aribella called.

'Probably to celebrate the flood passing and the sudden return of the Doge's health,' Clara replied. 'There'll be parties tonight! Oh, you won't *believe* how much I've missed rowing a gondola. You are pretty speedy, especially for a Novice! Let's see just how fast you can go. Race you to Burano!'

Aribella laughed and rowed as fast as her aching limbs would allow. They arrived at Papa's cottage breathless and exhilarated, their eyes shining.

When Papa opened the door, Aribella's heart leapt to see him safe. He looked thinner, but he was well and his face softened with happiness as he looked at Aribella. But when he caught sight of Clara, his eyes filled with astonished tears that began to pour down the lines on his face like rivers. Aribella had never seen Papa cry. In mourning, he'd been an empty shell, but he was not that person any more. It was as if he'd come alive again and all the tears he'd held inside for years were pouring out. He grabbed both of them, kissing Aribella's head and cheeks, before breaking down in Clara's arms.

'Oh, how are you both here? It is a miracle! Oh, Bella. Oh, Clara, my love. I couldn't . . . I couldn't cope without you.'

'Hush,' Clara soothed, tears falling from her eyes too. 'It's all right. Everything is fine now.'

They hugged each other tightly, squeezing Aribella between them. Aribella thought her heart might explode from happiness. It felt like the sweetest dream.

Eventually, Clara whispered, 'Ari, why don't you go and give Theo his gift now? Your papa and I have a lot to discuss.'

Aribella did not want to leave her parents ever again, but she knew their talk would be easier without her there, and she couldn't wait to see Theo. So she gave them both one final squeeze, and then ran down the street to Theo's cottage. She pummelled on the door, no longer afraid of who might see.

'Who's that?' Theo's papa appeared. 'Aribella?' He stared at her in surprise.

'Is Theo in?' she blurted.

'Yes, but I'm afraid he's had a rather rough night. He was caught in another storm out on the lagoon . . . He's lucky to be alive.'

'I know . . . I mean, can I see him, please?'

Theo's papa was eyeing her with distrust, but Aribella felt as if she was wearing a protective armour of joy. No one could ever make her feel like an outsider again.

'Who is it, Papa?' Theo appeared at the door.

'Theo!' Aribella exclaimed.

'Ari?' As soon as he saw her, Theo's face lit up and

he pushed past his papa and hugged her tightly. 'You're alive! I was so afraid. I had this rotten dream last night. It was really weird, so *real*. I dreamt we had this stupid fight on the lagoon and there was this horrible island . . . And I woke up thinking something awful had happened.' He shook his head. 'I'm just so pleased you're all right. Where have you been?'

'I've got something for you,' she said, dodging his question. 'Come with me!'

When Theo saw the gondolas at the harbour, his mouth hung open and he blinked very fast.

'Whose are they?' he gasped.

'One of them's yours. A gift.'

Theo's eyes widened. 'It can't be . . . You're winding me up.'

'I'm not.' Aribella grinned, pointing to the gondola that had been Ursula's.

Tentatively, Theo edged forward and ran his fingers along the smooth black hull. 'Where did you get it?'

Aribella shifted from one foot to the other. 'I can't really say.'

Theo turned back to face her, his forehead creased. She recognized the earnest look in his eyes. He was about to ask her something difficult. She steeled herself for hard questions, but what Theo said next surprised her.

'You don't have to tell me, Ari. I know that . . .

something is going on with you. I didn't get caught in a storm last night. I thought so at first, but then these other memories came back to me. They weren't a dream, I'm sure of it.'

So Marquesa was right; the Four Thieves Vinegar hadn't worked so well the second time. It had cleared the spectre bite, but not Theo's memory.

'You were there,' he continued, 'and *something* happened on the lagoon. Something bad . . . I won't tell Papa. Or anyone. But I know you saved me from something terrible. You came to help me when I needed you. And that's what matters. So, if you can't tell me, then don't. Just promise you won't disappear on me again.'

Aribella smiled. Oh, good, wonderful, kind Theo! Even now, when he was so bewildered, he was making things easier for her. She loved him so much it was like an ache deep inside her. She put her arm round his shoulder.

'I won't,' she promised.

Theo smiled. 'Friends?'

'No matter what,' she agreed firmly. She grinned at him. 'Want to take it for a spin?'

ribella went back to Burano often in the weeks that followed. Sometimes Seffie, Fin and Helena joined her.

Theo quickly warmed to her new friends and they spent long afternoons racing Theo's gondola (at Inbellis speed) around the lagoon before heading back to Papa and Mama's bright kitchen for dinner, or to Halfway though Theo never asked to join them there.

And one day there was a thick white envelope waiting for her on the reception desk. The envelope had her name written across it in swirling gold ink and there was a mask stamped into the purple seal. Rosa smiled as she handed the letter over.

With her heart beating very fast, Aribella tore the envelope open and read the letter inside.

Dear Aribella,

You are cordially invited to your mask fitting.

Please be prompt.

Tardiness is not tolerated.

Distinti saluti,

The Mask Maker (Mama)

That same afternoon, Aribella went to the shop and Clara – no longer a Mask Maker's apprentice – led her behind the black curtain into the bonding room. On the stand was a new mask. Patterns of orange, red and gold flames twisted across its face, and rubies, topaz and sapphires flickered and sparkled on its forehead. She recognized the mask instantly, like the face of an old friend, or a part of her own soul, staring back at her.

As Aribella met the mask's gaze, her fingers tingled and she felt something pass between her and the mask.

'Do you like it?' Clara asked.

'It's perfect,' Aribella whispered.

She reached for the mask and put it on. It felt light on her skin – not hot and clammy like the Mask of Venice, but as though she wasn't wearing a mask at all. As she tied the scarlet ribbons, she thought of Seffie, Fin and Helena, Rodolfo and Rosa. Mama and Papa. The Cannovacci and the Inbellis. The Halfway Hotel and Burano. Theo. All of them were part of Venice. Home.

And that, she realized with a joyful thump of her heart, was where she truly belonged.

Acknowledgements

It's such a huge moment to have *Aribella* published. A few key ingredients have made this possible: some blind faith, a great deal of stubbornness, and the support of fantastic people, without whom Aribella would still be hiding in Venice, so please indulge me while I thank a few of them.

My gratitude to Catherine Coe, who first saw magic under murky canal water. To my wonderful agent Caroline Walsh, for taking me on and her consistent support throughout all the ups and downs, also to Christabel for being such a fantastic cheerleader. To the Chickens: Barry, Jazz, Laura Smythe, Rachel Hickman, Elinor, Sarah, Lucy, Laura Myers and Kesia, for your hard work and expertise. Especially to Rachel Leyshon, for being a phenomenal editor and so kind and upbeat during the seemingly endless redrafts.

To Paola Escobar and Helen Crawford-White for the beautiful cover.

To the MAWFYP tutors: Julia, David, Steve, Janine and Lucy. The international writer's club: Anna, Imme and Laura especially, for keeping me sane during that year in L.A. To other workshop friends: Julie, Fin, Maddy, Mark, Dandy, Kirsty, Sue and Helen.

To Lucie, for all her support over the years. Hamish, I love you dearly, sorry I couldn't find a way to wangle the name 'Hamish' into an Italian story. Jess, Tom, Lucy, Abbi, Nelson, Chloe, Ed, Katie, Tim, Georgie H, Georgie W, Caroline, Portia, Roly, Harriet, Jemima, Teri, Johnny and Mia . . . and many more.

To early readers: Pat Ferguson and Karine Akande. To Oscar, Theo and Lola, aka the coolest kids on the planet, thanks for letting me read parts to you during nannying shifts. You are both wonderful company and brilliant reviewers!

To Granny Ireland, for inspiring me daily with her spirit, kindness and total love. To Granny H, for a childhood full of reading *Tintin* in bed. To my wonderful grandpas, who both loved stories, to Wilf, my aunts, Susie, Tracey and Isabelle, to Uncle Bob, and my excellent cousins: Sam, Olivia, Elsa and Hugo. To my fairy godmothers Sovra and Paula.

To Mum, for sobbing so much while reading me *The Amber Spyglass* that I learnt to read for myself just so I could find out what happened. To Dad, for your imagination and the example you set as a human being. You are both amazing parents and I am lucky to have you. To my sister Oni, for teasing me on pretty much everything except for my writing.

And to Chris, for everything. For being both my adventure and my home.

And finally, to you, reader, for picking up this book. I sincerely hope you enjoyed it. I know growing up can be a little tough, especially if you've not found the place you belong yet, but hold on and keep being true to yourself. Remember Rodolfo's words about the secret of being a misfit: you're never the only one. You will find people like you one day, people who make you feel like you don't need to be anyone but yourself. It might take months or years, and you might find them down the road or across the world, but they'll be there. Until then, there's no point wasting time pretending to be anyone except for who you are because one day you'll realize that what makes you different is your strength. Your *power*. So, don't let go of it.